This special signed
edition is limited to
1500 numbered copies
and 26 lettered copies.

This is copy __327__.

Colony High, BOOK ONE:

SKY HORIZON

David Brin

Illustrated by
Scott Hampton

Subterranean Press
2007

First Edition
ISBN-10: 1-59606-109-x
ISBN-13: 978-1-59606-109-5

Subterranean Press
PO Box 190106
Burton, MI 48519

www.subterraneanpress.com

Extra Credit

Rumors can take on a life of their own. Sometimes, they spread like a virus.

The latest bit of hearsay?

Some of the Math Club geeks have got a real live alien! Hidden in a basement rec room.

Mark had listened to some wild tales while growing up, wherever his father happened to be stationed at the time. Just as soon as he could pick up some of the local dialect, Mark would foray into the nearest village or town and tap the gossip mill, fascinated by the bottomless human appetite for preposterous lies. From conspiracy theories murmured in a Lebanese bazaar to scandals about local pop stars, circulating through Manilla alleys—the things people believed!

Still, it wasn't till Dad got transferred back to Southern California that Mark realized—there's no place better to breed wild stories than an American high school.

Especially Twenty-Nine Palms High, where the football team mascot, Spookie, wore a huge trench-coat, a floppy hat and big black mask. Beyond all the nasty stories that kids typically spread about each other, and hearsay concerning the dating habits of certain teachers, there were always colorful rumors about what went on at the nearby airbase. Or within the top-secret, opaque walls of Cirocco Labs.

But *this* one—about the Math Club guys having an extraterrestrial of their very own—beat all.

Not that Mark believed a word of it. *California homes don't have basements, for one thing.*

Besides. A captive alien?

Such a cliché. A stupid movie rip-off. Couldn't the nerds come up with a better hoax? Some of their parents worked at Cirocco, for pete sake. What good are brains if you can't be original?

When some of his classmates said they were going over to see for themselves, after school, Mark begged off. He had other things on his mind. Especially an hour later, staring down at the varsity soccer team—

—*girls* varsity, in blue shorts and yellow tops. They charged across the athletic field in formations as intricate as Dad's squadron during inspection week... but a whole lot more alluring. Somehow, they made sweat and cutthroat ferocity seem, well—

"Bam?" A voice called to him from above. *"Bamford, what are you doing?"*

The words made him twitch, almost losing his precarious perch upon a stub of concrete that jutted from the climbing wall. Mark dug in with three fingertips of his left hand, while probing desperately for a ledge to set his right foot. Heartbeats jolted and spots danced before his eyes like flashing balls.

"You all right? Bam?"

"Ye—yeah," he grunted, short of breath and embarrassed. "Slack... Gimme a lot."

Some tension left the rope, easing pressure from the climbing harness on his groin, freeing him to lean and traverse, seeking a higher footing. This part of the wall was tricky, designed for competitions in a brand-new league. He would have to master it in order to make the team.

"More slack!" The rope still wasn't loose enough for this reach.

"But..."

"Come on, Alex... I'm fighting the clock here. Slack!"

There was time to make up—precious seconds stupidly wasted during that blank stare at the soccer players. Damn hormones.

"Well, fine. But concentrate!"

The rope loosened still more. He bore down, focusing on the task at hand.

Relax, you're in a California desert suburb. This wall couldn't be any worse than that cliff in Morocco, when his father had to stay with a critically injured aid worker, sending Mark cross-country for help. One steep shortcut shaved an hour off the round trip... and Dad later blistered his ears over taking the risk.

The lip of Mark's left shoe found a crevice. Hardly more than a ripple in the wall. He tested it...

"That one's iffy," commented the voice overhead.

Be quiet. But he didn't have breath to say it. Shifting his weight onto the narrow ledge and feeling a sudden burn in his thigh, he launched himself upward, reaching ambitiously past a safe hand-hold, grabbing at the last one before the top. For an instant he glimpsed Alex, scowling with concern, her cropped brown hair framed by a blue desert sky.

This'll show her I know what I'm—

His hand brushed the knob—the same instant that his shoe slipped. Mark clutched frantically, two fingers bearing all his weight as both legs dangled, desperately seeking a purchase, anything at all. Specks of rough concrete crumbled under the pressure. Pain lanced down his wrist and arm.

"Mark!"

He saw Alex trying to reach for him, and suddenly remembered. *I asked for slack. I hope not too much—*

The knob seemed to tear away with deliberate malice—and the ground swung up, eager to smash. Mark glimpsed shouting figures below, scattering out of the way.

Almost too late, the autotensioner kicked in, yanking the

safety line hard enough to empty his lungs, stopping his plummet just short of impact.

For some unmeasurable time he hung there, tasting acid, blinking away pain-dazzles and struggling to catch his breath while Alex popped the release, easing him down the rest of the way.

Those scattered figures returned, crowding around as Mark's vision cleared—youths who were bigger, stronger and sweatier than most. Well, everyone agreed that the Climbing Wall stood too close to the Free Weights area.

The tallest body-builder leaned over, expressing false concern. "You okay there, Bamford? Want a pillow?"

Jeez. All I need right now is Scott Tepper, Mark thought.

And yet - there was no choice but to clasp the blond senior's offered hand. Better to stand quickly, ignore the pain and try not to groan, even if that meant swaying for several heartbeats.

"You're lucky Coach wasn't here," Scott continued, still looking down at Mark from half a head taller. "He's already ticked off that they put this stupid climbing wall here."

"Yeah," growled Larry Gornet, nearly as towering as Scott but much heavier, pushing close and poking with a finger. But that wasn't what made Mark recoil. The big lineman six-packed aroma.

"You could've killed somebody, Bamford! When Coach finds out, your 'ascent team' will be history."

Brushing Gornet's jabbing finger aside, Mark glanced at the nearest weight station. It lay at least three meters from the base of the wall. Plenty of room! He was about to argue the point when Scott Tepper raised a palm.

"No need for Coach to find out." He interposed, keeping Larry's persistent arm from poking again. A good thing, since Mark had had enough.

"But Scott, next time this moron falls..."

"There won't *be* a next time. Will there, Bamford?"

Mark couldn't think of anything to say. Though fuming inside, he knew it was a losing proposition to argue, or compete in any way with Scott Tepper, whose charm seemed to rise out of some infallible instinct. Coupled with good looks and serene confidence, it let Scott manipulate any teacher, win any school office, smooth-talk any girl.

So *much* confidence that he could offer generosity—at a price. *You owe me, Bamford,* said the look in Scott's eyes.

Others were joining the crowd of onlookers, including members of the girls soccer team. Helene Shockley, tawny and gorgeous, slid up next to Tepper with a questioning smile.

Mark shook his head, eager to get out of there.

"No, Scott. It won't happen again."

Alexandra Behr wasn't as easy to deal with.

"Do you have any idea how hard we lobbied Principal Jeffers to get that wall? It's our shot at getting some X-Sports accepted inside! You better not blow it for us, Bam."

Mark shot her a glare as they walked toward the bike racks. He'd never liked the nickname—*Bam-Bam...* later shortened to *Bam*—though its macho quality beat most alternatives. High school could be a social nightmare for any transfer student, especially if you got off on the wrong foot. Anyway, the Extreme Sports bunch had been first to accept him. Mark couldn't skateboard worth a damn, but none of *them* had ever gone trekking in the Atlas Mountains, so it all evened out. Why not help pioneer a new sport at TNPHS?

"It won't happen again," he told Alex.

This time the promise felt sincere. He *had* let her down, foolishly losing focus. In the real world, a slip like that could be fatal. Besides, he needed the ascent team, to boost upcoming college applications. Lacking Alex's grade point average, and a bit short for his age, this might be his one chance to varsity at anything.

"Well, okay then." Alex nodded, accepting Mark's word. She punched his shoulder, knowing uncannily how to strike a nerve.

He quashed a reflex to rub the spot.

Dang girls who take karate. Mark had grown up with the type, on a dozen military outposts around the world. Oh, they could be great pals. But a more feminine style also had appeal. Anyway, Alex was only a sophomore—not even sixteen and still gawky. Mark inclined toward 'older women' like Helene.

Unfortunately, *they* went for older guys.

Barry Tang awaited them at the bike racks, his Techno already unfolded with gleaming, composite wheels—hand-made for last year's Science Fair. With unkempt, glossy black hair and a mis-buttoned shirt, anyone could tell how he interfaced with Alex—on her non-athletic side. They were both Junior Engineers.

"What kept you two?" Barry asked, a little breathlessly. "I want to show you something!"

Mark groaned.

"Gimme a break, will you? My carcass is still practically twisted in half and covered with bruises. And I gotta be at work by four." Not that he relished bagging groceries. But Dad said any kind of job built character. In lieu of allowance, he pitched in a buck for every one Mark earned himself—mostly for the college fund.

"So? You've got twenty-three minutes, and Food King is right over there." Barry pointed to the supermarket, beyond Jonathan's Shell Station and across the street from Twenty-Nine Palms High.

"Well—"

"Come on, Bam." Alex took the back of Mark's neck with one strong hand and started kneading. "I'll work these knots, if you like."

He suppressed an impulse to brush her away. Alex was a pal, after all. Though every now and then…

"There," Barry shouted. "I see one!"

"See what?" Alex asked, releasing Mark's neck just when he was closing his eyes, ready to admit it felt good. By the time he looked up, both of his friends were pedalling ahead, past the alley where denim-clad bikers always hung out after tearing around on the dunes. Mark had to chase after, swerving to avoid a muttering bag lady's junk-laden shopping cart, barely catching his friends near the minimart on Main. Barry jabbed a finger north along Bing Crosby Boulevard, toward the Air Force base and a vast expanse of desert beyond.

"I don't see—"

"The van!"

Mark blinked. There *was* a van—dark blue, with windows tinted opaque gray. An oval area along one side had been painted over raggedly, without much effort to match colors. A tarp covered some kind of bulge on top.

"So? I don't see—"

"That color and model, I recognize it from the fleet at Cirocco Labs! There's at least a dozen—maybe more—cruising all over the place. Must've been in a real hurry. See how they just slapped some paint on the company logo? And I'll bet you that tarp's hiding sensors. Maybe some kind of a search radar!"

Barry looked so excited—and happy—that Mark hesitated to doubt him aloud. Especially when Alex cast a warning glance, shaking her head.

Is this going to be like a few months ago, when Barry kept yattering about giant Russian transport planes, landing in the middle of the night?

"Haven't either of you heard all the helicopters cruising overhead the last few days? I can spot *two* of em right now, from where we're standing! See that glint near the horizon?" He swiveled. "And there beyond the RV park, over Joshua Tree. They must be looking for something!"

Mark and Alex shared another glance. Neither of them had to say it. In Twenty Nine Palms, the sight of a military helicopter was about as surprising as spotting your own shadow. "A Marine exercise," Mark ventured. "Hotshots from Pendleton—"

"My parents *have* been nervous about something, the last few days," Alex murmured. "When I asked about it, they went all weird on me and clammed up."

Mark shot her an accusing look. *You too?*

Then something occurred to him.

I haven't seen Dad in two days.

Oh, that alone wasn't troubling. It happened several times a year. A note on the fridge, plus an envelope with some cash. No instructions. Just implicit confidence that Mark could be trusted to take care of himself for a while.

Only now he found himself worrying. *Could it be an alert?*

With so many hot spots in the world, units were always being called up and sent to far places that he'd never heard of, fighting in little scraps that never got called 'wars.'

He didn't recall anything in the news that seemed threatening. No looming crisis. But folks at the nearby base—and at Cirocco Labs—might be involved with something on the horizon, acting long before the media or public got wind of it.

"I joined the Math Club for a while, when I was a freshman," Barry said, his voice cracking slightly. "I still know a couple guys. We play chess now and then."

"So?" Mark just knew he was going to regret asking. Then the connection dawned on him…

…those silly rumors. *Oh, no.*

"So," Barry finished. "You guys want to find out what's going on?"

It turned into one hell of a Thursday night.

When Mark got off work around seven, he went home hoping to find his dad there, smelly and unshaven from a three-day field trial, but happy to tell his son all the unclassified parts over coffee and an omelette. Something that would explain all the eerie vans and nervous helicopters, even the bizarre rumors sputtering around town, putting it all down to scuttlebutt and normal Defense Department weirdness.

But no. Dad wasn't home.

Instead, Mark found Alex and Barry waiting for him by the battered old Cherokee. Barry held a steaming bucket of drumsticks. Alex must have already let herself in the house, to fetch keys to the jeep. She tossed them at Mark, as soon as he parked his bike.

"You don't waste time," he commented.

"Life's short." It pretty much summed up her philosophy.

What could he do but shrug and climb into the driver's seat? These two were his best friends since moving to this desert oasis. They had nursed him through those grueling Chemistry and Algebra II midterms, making it hard to refuse, even though his body ached and there was school tomorrow.

Piloting the Cherokee's stiff old suspension toward the north end of town—where the visitor from space was rumored to be hidden—Mark thought. *If true, it's the worst-kept secret since the Vice Principal got a hairpiece.*

He kept passing cars full of teens—some from TNPHS and others from Mojave College. It felt more like Saturday than a school night.

Alex waved at some guys wearing helmets and pads, who zipped along on gleaming pairs of sneaker skates—the latest fad—slower than cars, but a lot more fun and great for shortcuts whenever traffic got dense.

"Hey froggi. Sup!" Alex shouted as one of them came swooping by to slap a friendly palm on the Jeep's hood.

"Hey girl," the wiry boy answered as he spun around once then gave her fist a friendly punch. "Seen *it* yet?"

"It?"

"You know... *it!* Some of us are high on the waiting list. We're all taking bets, whether it's real."

"No way, man!" said another skater, barely missing a minivan that swerved into the left turn lane. Mark liked these guys, but they were crazier than kava-chewers.

"I bet it's a rubber puppet," the second one sneered. "Like that robotic thing, last Halloween."

"Yeah? Well Benny got close last night and he says—"

"Benny's mind is torqued from too much gaming, man. Can't tell what's real anymore. Come on, what're the odds?"

"Yeah but whatif? Sick! They're only letting a few visitors at a time and you gotta have cash. But I'll put in a good word for you, Alex. Maybe get your friends in—"

A warning bloop from a police car interrupted the skater, who shrugged with a blithe grin. Spinning 360, he vaulted the boulevard's center divider.

"Get us in *where?*" Alex shouted after him. But he was gone in a flash of turbo-luminescent rims. Cops didn't even bother chasing the X-guys anymore. They could dart through an intersection and vanish like smoke.

Something's up, all right, Mark thought as he followed Barry's hushed directions, along one dismally similar suburban side street after another. *The whole town feels it.*

Or at least the part that was tuned into coolstuf—the mesh of interests approved by those between fifteen and twenty. You didn't have to log into some avachat room to get a ruling on what's hot or not. It splattered like rain across *bboard* postings, a spray of half-sentence Instant Messages scrolling down specs and palm-pads. It murmured into earpieces and swarmed over the foldscreens or pullscreens of countless cell phones.

Pretty sharp, Mark admitted, grudgingly. Whatever it turned out to be—probably a hoax—somebody deserved credit for the town's best mob-ilization since he had arrived. Even better, the world of adults appeared clueless. So far, this whole thing seemed limited to the young.

I take that back, Mark thought suddenly, pulling the jeep over to one side. Just ahead, a police car had parked along the very block where Barry said the vice-president of the Math Club lived. Two officers were just getting out, slamming doors.

With a hiss, the black-haired boy pointed.

"Look. There's *two* of those disguised Cirocco vans, just pulling up!"

"This is creepy," Alex said. A crowd was gathering, mostly teens, milling about and peering at the house in question.

"What do we do? Take a look? Someone outside may know—"

Someone rapped hard on the right-rear door. Barry yelped as pale face suddenly pressed against the glass, fogging it with hasty breath.

"Tang! Thank god it's you. Open up!"

"What in—" Mark didn't have time to object as Barry let in a figure, swaddled by a cowled windbreaker.

"Drive!" the boy croaked.

"But—"

"Get out of here! Then I'll explain."

Against his better judgement, Mark put the car in gear, turning carefully so as not to attract attention. His uninvited passenger sighed, quivering as he looked back at the commotion.

"Alex and Mark, this is Tom," said Barry. "Tom Spencer. That was *his* house with the police car in front."

Alex reached around, offering her hand to the nervous sophomore. "What's up? Want something to drink? We have Pepsi. Or a drumstick?"

Good move, Mark approved, offering a frightened person something as commonplace as food. Though he kept blinking rapidly, the Spencer kid seemed to calm a bit as he slurped a can of soda.

"They… came less than an hour ago. Just busted right in and *took* him!"

"Who came? The police? Didn't they just arrive?" Alex stayed scrupulously calm as the boy shook his head.

"Jocks! It was Larry Gornet and some of his football pals!" In the rear-view, Mark saw Tom take another long slurp, before resuming his rapid babble. "They came by for the first time last night, polite as could be. Paid me *fifty dollars* to let them in. Just wanted to have a look, they said. I should've listened to Dwight. He told me not to! But fifty will help buy that new hacking algorithm I wanted all year. So I let 'em in." He slapped the dashboard, reverberating the Jeep's rickety cab. "Idiot!"

"Chill, Tom. You say they paid you to let them look at something. *What* did they pay to see?"

But he was chattering now, telling it his own way.

"By this morning, it seemed like every kid in town knew! People kept sneaking up to my back door after school, offering *more* cash for a look at Xeno. It felt cool for a while, till Gornet and his bunch came back. They crashed right in and grabbed him!"

"Who did they grab?"

Tom Spencer shook his head.

"Then it got worse! My parents heard us yelling as Gornet left. They saw Gavin's black eye and found the mess downstairs… *so they called the cops.* I couldn't stop them!"

Mark shook his head. Clearly this dude had a hierarchy of fears. Invasion by thieving athletes was intolerable—but not *half* as bad as alerting the world of adults.

"All right," Alex asked. "You're saying Gornet and his pals came barging in and grabbed someone. But who, Tom? Who did they take?"

Mark found himself fervently hoping that Tom would just shut up.

It's just a hoax that got out of hand, he hoped. *It's got to be.*

Tom swallowed hard before answering.

"They took our xenoanthropoid."

"Your—?"

Barry Tang translated. "It's Greek, meaning 'something like a manlike being from beyond.' Pretty awful Greek, actually. I guess they wanted something less cliched than *alien* or *extraterrestrial.*"

Tom sniffed.

"We spent days coming up with that! Anyway, it's a damn good thing we were the ones who found him. Well, Julie Mendel did, while she was performing one of her routine comet-searches. The IR scanner on her 22-inch wide-field telescope spotted something coming in fast."

"Nobody at the base saw it?"

"Her correlator noticed something all those Cirocco brainiacs missed!" Tom snorted, both proud and contemptuous. "I guess because it had all the color values of a falling meteorite. Anyway, a fresh carbonaceous chondrite is worth heaps, so Julie called me and Dwight and Gavin and Lauren to check the fall site, out in the southern drifts. Only when we got there, we found..." The boy's hands shook as he gestured, shaping something rounded, almost as if he could still see it, right in front of his face.

"... we found a *space capsule of some kind,* half imbed-ded in one of the dunes!"

"No way!" Barry sighed, in a tone that was almost reverent and hushed. He prompted. "Then—"

"Then we found *him*... wandering around on the sands."

Mark shook his head as he drove, silently wishing.

Please make it stop.

Oh, part of him shared the excitement, a natural yearning for something exceptional to happen. Something more interesting than the semi-rural ennui of typical American teenage life, spent largely warehoused in a high school regimen that often seemed to have no other purpose than taking up time, keeping youths occupied at an age when biology made them want to *move!* To experience and have adventures. In other eras there had been frontiers and unknown lands to dream about. Today?

Small wonder that first-contact with some kind of alien race was the stuff of so many movies and modern legends—occupying a place in modern hearts that used to be devoted to mythological beasts and exotic foreign princesses.

But really, how likely was it for some star- visitor to show up right now? Science had never found a single trace of intelligent life. No radio messages from the stars, nor any verifiable evidence of visits to Earth, not even in the planet's deep past.

None of this made sense.

Why here? Why now?

"So you took this... entity to your basement." Alex summarized, her voice low and disbelieving.

"After burying the capsule." Tom Spencer nodded. "My rec room seemed best, since my parents never come down there. Boy, was *that* an all-nighter! But by morning Julie had him surrounded with a kick-ass audio-visual translation system. We tried every language you can download from the Web."

"How'd that go?" Barry asked eagerly.

"Not so good. So we backtracked and started over with per-mutation math. You know, universal stuff that any technological species oughta know. There are even some programmed scenarios, pre-worked out by amateur SETI clubs—"

"And?" Barry was barely touching his seat from excitement.

"And? Well, I gotta admit things got pretty frustrating! None of the stuff we downloaded seemed to work. None of the math or geometry or symbol stuff. Or web picture shows. For one thing, we had trouble getting Xeno's attention. He wasn't in great shape. Gavin offered all kinds of food. Thank God he took a sudden liking to marrow."

"Marrow?"

"The stuff inside bones, that makes red blood—"

"We know what marrow is," Mark snapped. He was starting to get angry. And he realized something else.

I've been driving without thinking...

...toward Larry Gornet's house.

It was in the best neighborhood of Twenty-Nine Palms—sometimes called "New Palm Springs"—where spacious homes sprawled amid heaps of non-native greenery... lush plants and trees that drank water by the acre-foot. He knew the place with a nagging sense of personal hurt. Shortly after Mark transferred to TNPHS, someone ambiguously invited him to drop by one of Gornet's parties, where kids at the top rung would be hanging out. Swallowing the bait, he showed up only to be turned away at the door amid raucous laughter from those inside.

Sure, he should have seen the sucker-draw miles away. *My own damn fault, if it hurt.*

Anyway, never mind all that. What bothered Mark right now was a sense of consistency to this story. If Gornet and his pals really had taken something—or some*body*—from the math nerds, it would be completely in character.

Still, Mark felt little sympathy for Tom Spencer.

"Why?" he asked. "Why keep a space alien in your basement?"

"Because I'm the only one who *has* a basement. It's roomier than Gavin's shed and warmer at night. Didn't I just say that my folks never go down there—"

A frustrated gurgle filled Mark's throat. With a glance his way, Alex took over.

"No, Tom. The question is—why didn't you *call* somebody? NASA. The Air Force. The State Department. The press?"

Tom blinked, as if unsure he could be hearing her right. As if the question made no sense at all.

"But... but... he's ours!"

For a slender youth, Tom's jaw set with grim determination.

"He's ours, and we're gonna keep him."

Once Tom got started, there were plenty of rationalizations.

"We hid Xeno in order to save his life! Those government guys would only dissect him the minute they got their hands on him."

Sure, Mark thought sarcastically as he swung into Bryer Estates. *Cut up a star-alien. You'll learn lots that way. More than, say, by asking questions.*

But Tom wasn't finished.

"Those guys would just take him to some secret underground lab and hide him forever!"

Again, Mark shook his head silently.

Maybe. But to study an alien technology you'd need hundreds of skilled people—maybe thousands—the very best, with open minds. The kind of top professionals who inherently question assumptions and resent needless secrecy.

What's to stop any of them from leaking proof of a coverup?

It was always the same with all UFO or "Roswell" type cult stories. They invariably assumed that the very brightest members of a free society were all drones and fools and tools.

Mark envisioned someone trying to cram *Dad* into a category like that. *Yeah, right.*

"The government would *have* to keep this kind of thing hidden from the public," went Tom's next rationalization, one that he clearly must have rehearsed among his friends.

"The potential for mass hysteria is unimaginable!"

Now he's quoting from some movie, Mark thought.

Funny how everybody is always sure that their own in-group can handle disturbing news, but that people in general would riot or go mad.

Sure, I'm kind of shocked—but I also feel… focused. Either this is a great big hoax, designed to make the whole town look stupid, or—

—or else our entire world may be changing.

Either way, it kind of gets your attention.

By the time they parked, three doors from the stately Gornet home, Tom Spencer was fizzing with schemes to win back what had been taken from him. For starters, he wanted Alex and Barry to contact the other Young Engineers.

"We mathists should've included you guys from the start," he confessed. "With all those gladiator robots you techies keep building, it should be a cinch to break into Gornet's place. Then pow!" He punched the air. "But first we gotta reconnoiter."

"Gotta what?"

"Check the grounds, figure a way in. Julie has some great night vision equipment. Let's head over to her place and.... hey! Where are you going?"

Mark stepped out of the Jeep, closing his door softly behind him.

"We're going to *reconnoiter*, like you said," Alex said, following Mark's example as Tom sputtered and started to protest. Barry grabbed the Spencer boy's shoulder and he lapsed into silence, trailing nervously a few paces behind.

The pavement felt strangely gritty under Mark's feet. Pebbles scraped louder, more vividly than normal, like the hissing sprinklers on a nearby lawn. Mark recognized the sensation. Adrenaline rush. The senses can heighten astoundingly when your comfortable routine has been shattered, replaced by daunting flickers of a new—and possibly hazardous—unknown.

He wondered. Did people feel this way all the time in olden-tribal days, back when the surrounding night held fearsome mysteries, anything from hungry tigers to angry gods? This level of heightened awareness could be dreadful... or *exhilarating*, an ultimate high. No wonder so many kids were drawn to taking risks. A more natural and thrilling high than any drug.

And yet, most of these high schoolers don't know a thing about real danger, he thought as he led their foursome along the shadowed rim of a long, sweeping driveway. *Most people learn about trouble from movies.*

Mark had some first-hand experience with the real thing. Like that time in Bolivia, when his father's training unit wasn't supposed to bring dependents into a territory known for kidnappings and militia-style killings. But Mom had just passed away and Dad didn't want to leave a grieving boy behind, to fester with aunts and uncles. So he swung a student exchange program for Mark in La Paz. Safe enough, it seemed. That is, till Mark and a local kid took that impulsive drive into the mountains, and everything suddenly got intense....

The Gornet house was a rambling thing built during the recent land boom, when Cirocco Labs set up shop nearby. It was made up of several structures linked by fancy, glassed-in walkways—great for formal entertaining. And for keeping bothersome teenagers out of the way around back, where a large guest cabaña stood next to the blue ripple of a huge swimming pool. Mark quickly spotted other kids from TNPHS hanging about, small clusters of seniors and juniors mostly, talking in hushed, excited tones. Cigarette embers flared, here and there, like jittery fireflies.

Mark recalled the last time he came to this place. There had been loud music and a lot less tension in the air. Still, he felt wary.

Could this be another trap? A hoax, designed to draw in whole groups of suckers at a time, like an assembly line? An impressive stunt can make your senior class a legend, recalled with envy by generation after generation of students at Twenty-Nine Palms High.

He glanced suspiciously at Tom Spencer, who might be playing a pivotal role, lending credibility to the spoof. The fifteen-year old honors student licked his lips nervously. His earlier look of combative determination was giving way to anxiety.

Could he be acting?

Maybe. If it was Drama Club instead of Math Club. But I'd bet any chance I'll ever get a sports car that he's genuinely scared right now. And pissed-off over losing something precious.

An alien? Maybe not. Probably not. But something.

Mark and Alex walked past several of the small groups. Eyes flitted and crossed, without anyone offering a challenge. Not so far.

They approached within spitting distance of the cabaña before two large figures emerged from a heavily curtained doorway. One of them thrust out a burly arm.

"Close enough. You brats got cash? There's a cover."

"A c-cover?" Barry asked. "How much?"

"A hundred just to go in. Twenty a minute for a closer look."

Ouch! Mark thought. He had just the price of one admission in the envelope Dad left behind. *So it is a scam, after all. Whether the story's true or not.*

"What?" Tom Spencer stepped forward angrily, briefly forgetting his fear. "I let five of you in at once, for just fifty!"

The taller figure—Mark recognized one of the school running backs—shrugged with indifference. "We've got expenses. It costs a lot to keep a specimen like this. Call it a contribution for upkeep."

"Specimen?" Tom squeaked. "He's an intelligent life form! You're not only thieves. You'll be *murderers* if you keep this up. You don't have any idea what you're doing!"

Another form stepped out of the dimly-lit guest house. This time, Mark recognized Larry Gornet, dressed in khakis and a black turtleneck. He felt Tom Spencer go suddenly iron-tense... only to jolt back in surprise at Gornet's mild, offhand tone.

"Hey Spencer. I'm glad you came. Sorry things got a little rough at your house. But you were talking stupid and we had to act fast. Anyway, we need to talk some more. Right now."

Gornet barely glanced at Mark, Alex and Barry. "Your friends can go right in, to make sure the xeno-thing is all right."

He assumes we're members of Tom's bunch, Mark realized, unsure whether to feel glad or insulted over being mistaken for one of the Math Club domes.

Stunned by Gornet's sudden cordiality, Tom stared up blankly as a beefy hand took his arm, leading him over to the pool. Soon he was nodding as the big senior spoke, motioning repeatedly toward the guest house.

"Come on." Barry tugged at Mark and Alex. "Before they change their minds!"

The door guardians scowled at the idea of giving out freebies.

"Don't throw anything or raise your voices," one of them warned, holding back a thick curtain for Mark and the others to enter. "And the next guy who pokes it with a stick is gonna be sorry."

Mark's eyes took some time adjusting to the dim light inside, made even more difficult by a single pinpoint, glaring from one corner of the room. The source, a small but intense spotlight, shone outward from a large cage—the sort made for big dogs in a kennel.

Moving closer, he sniffed fresh redwood shavings... then a musty, wet smell of uncooked meat... and finally something else. An aroma unlike anything he ever encountered in his travels.

The cage had some furnishings. Two television sets flickered with the sound turned down low, one of them showing a children's cartoon program while the other featured some kind of stock car demolition derby. Paper and crayons lay untouched on a low table. Mark noticed what looked like the remains of a laptop computer in one corner, broken into several pieces.

Alex nudged him toward the opposite end of the enclosure. Mark had to force his reluctant body, head, and gaze to turn.

A shape stirred there, about the size of a ten year-old child—or maybe a chimpanzee. There was something hunched-over about its posture. Clutching a shrouding blanket, like a monk's hood, it moved from the far corner as Mark squinted past the glare. The figure slowly reached out to take something from a greasy platter. Droplets of dark, dense moisture fell audibly.

Till that moment, part of Mark had nursed a fading hope that it would all turn out to be a hoax after all, a truly first-rate *gotcha*, so clever that you'd tell your kids about it someday, proud even to be one of the dumb suckers who fell for it.

Meanwhile, another part yearned for everything to be true! Something both dazzling and different to shake up this dreary suburban life. A thrill of recognition and affinity with the strange. He had felt it before, in other lands, finding things in common with people who spoke exotic tongues in far corners of the globe.

One or the other. A grand hoax or a startling new connection. Either would be fine.

But then Mark watched that arm extend, grabbing a hunk of raw meat, and he knew.

It's got two elbows on each arm. Just one joint on each finger.

And that's not like any skin I ever saw.

And there's nobody this side of Hollywood who could fake moves like that.

A big, dripping rib-eye steak lifted from the platter and vanished under the blanket. There were crunching sounds…

…then a gobbet of chewed-up meat and bone hurtled toward a nearby bucket, already brimming with bloody detritus.

"Yikes," Alex said.

"It—it *can't* be real," Barry stammered, though he had been the most enthusiastic up till that moment.

Then the makeshift hood slipped back. From under the blanket emerged a tapered snout, tinged red. It moved in a side-to-side chewing motion that Mark could not remember ever seeing on Animal Planet. The skull was very wide and flat on top. Two forward-facing eyes bulged from either side of the extended jaw. They glittered in the spotlight, with a golden quality that Mark didn't find either warm or cheering.

A faint *chuttering* sound emerged. Strange and unhappy. Or at least, that was how it felt. Then a greasy hand stretched toward them. A multi-digited hand extended, pointing.

It could be asking for help, Mark speculated. *Or saying 'I'll remember your faces.'*

Or that could be a polite gesture where he comes from, meaning 'thanks for all the yummy steaks.'

Or else, he thought, watching the finger twitch at each of them in turn, *maybe that sound is its way of saying 'Bang, bang!'*

Mark tried to quash feelings of revulsion that welled from the pit of his stomach. According to the movies, aliens came in five varieties, monstrous, sexy, silly, wise or adorable... or some combination of those clearcut traits. They were supposed to rouse simple emotions—attraction, pity, giggles, awe or dread.

Off-hand, he couldn't recall portrayals of anything like this—so ambiguously weird, so pathetic and dauntingly at the same time...

...but also kind of gross.

That was what finally convinced him it couldn't be a ruse. Nobody would try so hard to fake a creature that filled you with confusion. The old cliches—even terror—were more comforting and credible.

Everybody has a coping mechanism. Alex seeemed to take refuge in dispassionate scrutiny.

"Binocular vision," she mused. "Very widely spaced hunters' eyes. I'd guess nocturnal predator ancestors..."

It was the sort of thing Mark might have expected Barry Tang to say. But under stress, it was all Barry could manage just to stammer.

"I can't decide... w-whether to laugh or hurl."

Mark nodded, agreeing.

Just don't do both at the same time.

"All right, that's enough," growled a voice behind them. "You can see he's doing just fine. Now you nerds get out."

Mark and Alex had to drag at Barry till his gaze broke from the creature in the cage. "Wait," he babbled. "There's got to be... some kind of explanation...."

And he was right. An explanation of a sort awaited them outside, where a suddenly eager Tom Spencer could be seen shaking Larry Gornet's hand. As Gornet turned to stride toward the big house, Tom actually beamed.

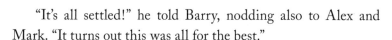

"It's all settled!" he told Barry, nodding also to Alex and Mark. "It turns out this was all for the best."

"What do you mean?" Alex asked.

"I mean we should have listened to Larry in the first place! This town is getting way too hot, with all those Cirocco guys prowling around suspicious. We've got to move Xeno, quick! Anyway this is going to require a lot more resources than Julie and Gavin and I could manage by ourselves. Larry's got contacts in Los Angeles, where you can hide anything! He knows one of the actors on *Rock n' Troll* who has his own place in Bel Air, without interfering parents—"

"But—"

"Larry says *we* can stay in charge of the scientific side, figuring out Xeno's needs and working on a translation program. He and his friends will take care of logistics and finance."

Like charging big-time admission to some highly-selected urban elite, Mark thought, picturing how this could vault Gornet into partying with Hollywood's bad-boy aristocracy. What better ticket than offering jaded stars something secret and new? Something truly out-of-this-world.

Plus maybe the lion's share of any fantastic reward that may come from assisting a stranded alien to find its way back home. Isn't that the classic scenario? Help it escape the vile grownups who run government and civilization and you'll get a magic ring or sword or something.

The payoff could be limitless.

"But first, we've got to get him out of town!" Tom babbled. "Larry's arranging transportation to a better hiding place—"

Alex blurted, "You've got to be—" but stopped short when Mark took her elbow. It was time to listen.

"*We've* got to work on erasing the trail!" Tom continued. "That means coming up with a believable cover story. So we've decided to pretend it was all a prank all along!"

"Um… how do you plan to do that?" Mark asked.

"Oh, it shouldn't be too hard. We'll set up something here in the cabaña… some kind of *fake* alien that moves a bit and makes some noise… anything to explain the rumors, convince eyewitnesses they were fooled in the dark. That's where your Engineer Club pals come in, Barry. Can you get a team together and come up with something by morning? Larry promised to cover your expenses!"

Barry blinked a few times, warming to the notion.

"We-e-ll… I think so. Nothing fancy. But now that I think about it, we got a bunch of actuators and stuff left over from Halloween… and I know where to get some of that Plastic Flesh goo they use on mobile store mannequins. It won't match the real thing. A lot of guys will remember the difference."

"Let em. That's the beauty of it! Wild stories are just fine. Let people yell coverup all they want. The whole thing could even wind up on some UFO show, like *Mysteries of the Weird!* Won't matter a bit, so long as we make the hoax explanation seem plausible. It'll be enough to throw off the scent!"

While Tom and Barry babbled more about how to build a fake alien in just a few hours, Mark glanced toward the big house. Through a downstairs window, he saw Larry Gornet in a room plastered with music and sports posters, talking urgently on his cell phone. Others paced and smoked, making calls of their own. A lot of organizing seemed to be going on. No surprise there. American teens who could not manage simple algebra could nevertheless be amazingly capable at coming up with highly sophisticated plans. At least when it came to things they cared about—from arranging elaborate parties or vacation trips to running a student election.

Or else pulling something over on clueless parents. No scholastic test could appraise such skills. They formed out of life experience, the way young cavemen would have learned about prey animals or the lay of the land.

Mark glimpsed Scott Tepper and Helene Shockley, using their own phones on a sofa. So, the very top layer of TNPHS society was involved. In fact, Tepper may have been using Gornet as a front man, pulling the real strings all along.

And now, by pure chance, Alex and I are being invited to participate, Mark realized. Maybe two dozen would finally wind up inside. Too many to keep a secret, normally. But with the tribal gulf between generations—helped by a sense of drama and Tepper's charismatic leadership—the conspiracy might hold together. For a while. Long enough to get something going in LA.

Maybe.

Well, you wanted something special in your life. Something exciting.

He had yearned to be accepted. Nothing was more likely to guarantee it than helping Tepper and Gornet spirit away a creature from the stars, stashing the thing safely in some urban hideaway, then assisting Barry and his friends as they focused their considerable talents on talking to the alien-guest. While a vast majority at TNPHS scratched their heads in wonder at tonight's 'hoax', Mark would be part of the core group, right there with Tepper and beautiful Helene, doing something sensational, amazing, important....

That final word made him blink.

Important...

... important to who?

While Barry and Tom argued about which supplies might be needed, and whose talents were absolutely essential to the conspiracy, Mark couldn't help remembering that ugly thing under the blanket, at once both pathetic and chilling. Intelligent. And definitely alive.

He thought again about his own excitement over being part of something dramatic, secretive and bold. It was alluring— almost too good to be true.

Question the very thing you want to believe.

He once saw that motto in a most unlikely place, carved on the lintel over a modest doorway, in a small Mauritanian curio shop. The Arabic expression had taken root somewhere in his brain, now rising up to haunt him.

We're thinking about what's important to us.

To us.

But we don't really matter right now.

In fact, what I want is just about the least important thing in the world.

Mark turned and took Alex's arm, retreating a few steps toward the shadowed drive.

"We've got to talk."

She met his gaze straight-on. And though her face didn't mesmerize him the way Helene Shockley's did, he found something much more helpful right now in her eyes—common sense.

"Are you thinking what I'm thinking?" she asked.

He couldn't bring himself to come right out and say it. The plan forming in his mind right now would finish him, socially, at Twenty-Nine Palms High School. Worse, it would follow him wherever he went, branding him from tonight onward.

Still, he kept picturing the creature in the cabaña, pointing that crooked finger and chuttering strange, alien phrases.

And Mark recalled something else... something that Clint Eastwood had said, in one of those timeless Dirty Harry movies.

"A man's got to know his limitations," he murmured out aloud.

Alex shot him a questioning look. And Mark shook himself.

"Let's go. We have work to do."

Homework ⟨ **2** ⟩

In the days that followed, Mark's heart sank with every news report that mentioned his name. Reporters haunted the front lawn, shouting questions whenever he came outside. Every time the phone rang, he felt a tightness in his throat.

Fortunately, Dad handled most calls—the obscene or threatening ones, along with those who offered help. "No, we don't need police protection," Mark heard him tell the County Sheriff at one point. "I've been given a desk job till this blows over—paperwork I can handle mostly from home. So just leave all the cranks and drive-bys to me. They're mostly blowhards."

Maybe. But some of the phone voices were pretty scary, whispering or shouting threats... or else making dumb fake-alien noises. Mark didn't bother checking email anymore. His in-box overflowed with messages from all over the world—some approving, but all-too many of them anonymous denunciations, expressing ALL-CAPS fury over what he he'd done.

"You don't have to go on limited duty," Mark told his father, who was already in uniform, despite the fact that he'd be working from home today. "Your unit has an important job, now more than ever. I can stay. Watch things here—"

"—and skip school? Not likely." Major Bamford chuckled. "Look, son, I know some jerks may be rough on you today. But you've got to face them. What you did was smart and brave. You thought about humanity and your country, not just a circle of delusional teens. It was the right thing to do."

The right thing?

Maybe. But also painful. At Mark's age, there were few put-downs more devastating than to be called a 'snitch'. Even among those who agreed with his decision, many thought that Mark did it out of self-interest—to grab headlines and become the center of attention. That opinion only grew each time his photo appeared in newspapers or the web.

None of the stories got it right of course, or told how difficult the choice had been.

"Go on," his father told him that morning, eighty hours after a fateful Thursday night. "Go to school. Try to have a normal day."

Easier said than done. But Mark knew that he meant well, and Dad's approval mattered more than anyone else's. *Especially since it might just be the two of us again, if I have to transfer schools. Or leave town.*

That seemed increasingly likely, from the moment he swung his bike into the racks at TNPHS, feeling intense looks from everyone he passed. Conversations died whenever he drew near. A few kids smiled nervously. But a larger number scowled at the infamous traitor who had turned 'their' xeno over to the Feds. No matter that most of the students had never heard of it till the news broke on Friday. Not even the latest reports—about improvements in the star-visitor's health and progress in crossing the language divide—seemed to make much difference in the mood on campus. The alien was now part of the greater world, and this place was just another drab American high school again.

It got worse indoors. Soon he couldn't take more than a dozen paces without hearing someone *horking* in the back of their throat, as if preparing to spit. It became a theme song, following him around. When Mark reached his locker and spied a greasy brown fluid leaking out the bottom, he decided not to bother opening it, denying any satisfaction to those who were watching.

A crowd had gathered at the door to history class. Any hope of slipping inside and quietly taking his seat was dashed when yet another news crew emerged from the room, pushed by an affably insistent Mr. Clements, wearing his typical striped shirt and colorful tie. Hot camera lights made beads of sweat shimmer on his peaked, receding hairline.

"Enough please! We're serious students and educators here. Save your questions for off-hours. Anyway, I was just a witness. The real heroes…"

Mark tried to melt into the crowd, but Mr. Clements spotted him first.

"Well, speak of the young man himself. Here's Mark Bamford, the fellow who invited me to participate in last Thursday's adventure."

Mark winced when he saw the camera crew was from Channel Ten, one of the local stations that missed out on the 'adventure' when they refused his invitation, dismissing him as a crank. A costly mistake, and now they seemed eager to take revenge by painting Mark in the worst possible light, making up ridiculous motives.

That he hoped for a reward from the government.

That he was taking revenge for a romantic disappointment.

That he had religious objections to aliens.

That he was already talking to Hollywood agents. (A few had, indeed, called and left messages—Mark had no intention of answering.)

None of the reporters told the truth about those frantic hours he and Alex had spent on that nervous Thursday evening, trying to set things up just right. They had to act fast. Scott Tepper and Tom Spencer—leading a their strange, jock-nerd alliance—were already gathering a caravan of private vehicles, preparing to transport the xeno off to some hip refuge deep inside the LA sprawl, rationalizing to themselves that they were doing *something heroic,* defending a 'guest' from the vile-distrusted government.

Oh, it would have been easy enough just to foil their crazy plan. If that was all he and Alex wanted, they had only had to phone up the Air Force. Or Cirocco labs.

But that option rasied worries of its own. Did it make sense to transfer custody of the castaway from one group of secretive paranoids to another? Tom Spencer had a point. Some clique of bureaucratic poobahs would surely talk themselves into thinking just like Scott and Gornet! Foolishly trying to hide all evidence of an extraterrestrial encounter, keeping in to an elite in-group, and coming up with elaborate reasons to justify it to themselves.

The world has plenty of bright fools in it, eager to act out movie cliches.

Oh, the secret probably wouldn't hold for very long, which-ever group tried. Mark doubted that any cover story could last in today's world. Take the crazy notion that three generations of top savants had been studying a spacecraft that crashed at Roswell, New Mexico, ever since 1949.

Right. Hundreds of scientists and engineers, investigating fantastic alien technologies—with none of them blabbing in all that time? Not even when they retired? Nobody who actually knew a living, breathing scientist would believe such nonsense. The best minds are independent; the very trait that made them "best." Even a military man like Dad would eventually get fed up with secrecy that stretched on and on, for no apparent reason. Especially if it appeared also to violate the law.

And nowadays, secrets can leak, 'accidentally', by as many paths as there are addresses on the internet.

Still, some group of adult-Gornets might decide to try. In fact, given human nature, the odds were better than even that they would.

So, for two wild hours, Mark and Alex made calls and pounded on doors, collecting nearly a dozen reputable witnesses, then driving around—with several of them fuming impatiently—till the moment seemed right to dial up Cirocco.

As he elbowed his way into the classroom, ignoring Channel Ten's shouted questions, Mark found himself almost wishing he never made that call—even though the plan worked better than he or Alex could have hoped.

Cirocco spooks responded to his anonymous tip with startling speed. A little after midnight, three blue vans swept into Bryer Estates, roared up the Gornets' ornate driveway and pinioned a surprised Tom Spencer with their headlights as black-swaddled men leaped out, carrying sophisticated gear...

...only to be surprised in turn when Mark pulled in behind them, blocking their exit! The witnesses that he and Alex had invited hopped out, covering *both* groups with spotlights and digicams, transmitting live to the world.

The government agents had no choice then, but to identify themselves. To show credentials and do it all on video, while the juniormost anchor from Channel Six babbled excitedly, no doubt with visions of national promotion dancing in her eyes.

Poor Tom and his friends wailed when they saw their 'xenoanthropoid' led gently out of the cabaña, into an air-conditioned van. The jocks—including Larry Gornet—were quieter in their disappointment—(goodbye Hollywood starlets!)—though Mark felt several of them drilling him with vengeful expressions.

He had managed to stand erect and met their gaze, remembering what Tom Spencer himself said, just a few hours before.

You'd be murderers if you kept this up.

You just don't have any idea what you're doing.

Now, as he sat at his usual desk in history class, Mark realized.

I didn't either.

It took Mr. Clements ten minutes to get rid of the TV people—maybe he wasn't trying all that hard—and to settle class back to any semblance of a normal routine, taking roll and collecting the weekend's essay assignment about the European Sixty Years War.

The teacher shook his head at the skimpy pile. Mark's contribution amounted to just two pages, rehashed from a single Wikipedia article. In big type, with generous margins.

"Now people," Mr. Clements said. "I know there have been some distractions lately, but that's no excuse for slacking off. In fact, this startling news about First Contact ought to emphasize the need for *focus*. What event could possibly make clearer the importance of education for your future?"

A hand shot up from the forward right. Dave McCarty, wearing his usual black leather jacket, spoke without waiting to be called.

"Why?" he asked, pushing contemptuously at the textbook in front of him. "Everything we know is obsolete! All our technology, science, arts... it's passé. In a few years we'll be using teleportation and warp drives, learning whatever we want from pills!"

That drew laughter. But many classmates also nodded.

"So," Mr. Clements asked. "Should we dismiss our old-fashioned schools till then?"

"Sure! Why waste brain cells studying stuff we'll never need?"

"Even the history of your species and civilization?"

"*Especially* history. It's irrelevant. Everything before now will be remembered as a time of primitives, like cavemen. B.C... for Before Contact!" McCarty chortled, clearly feeling he was on a roll.

"And do the rest of you feel the same way?"

Silence. Mark, especially, didn't want to attract any more attention. Anyway, he wasn't sure he disagreed with Dave.

Mr. Clements walked around the desk and put his hand on a Earth globe that always stood there.

"I'll grant you, it seems like a pretty small place in a big universe right now," he mused. "Though our ancestors thought it was vast and filled with dark unknowns." He set the globe spinning.

"Take for example the period we've been studying, the Sixteenth and Seventeenth Centuries—"

Students groaned. This teacher would use any excuse to swerve back on course.

"—a time of wrenching transition, perhaps even more shattering than the one we are about to enter."

Hodge Takahashi snorted from a seat in back.

"How could anything compare with *first contact?* To meet powerful aliens with incredible technologies you don't understand—"

"Exactly!" Mr. Clements grinned. And he waited. One of his famous pauses. Which usually meant that something—some connection—had been made. One that should be obvious to anyone who was paying attention.

Amid the ensuing hush, Mark felt a sudden wrench of understanding. *Oh,* he thought.

Almost against his will, Mark's hand started to raise… but another voice spoke up first.

"People in Africa… and Asia and the Americas… that was the very time when *they* had to adapt to strange new things—to *aliens*—when they faced European invaders."

Mark turned around to see Helene Shockley, sitting to his left and two chairs back. As usual, she was simply overwhelming. With black hair falling in ringlets over dusky shoulders. To Mark's surprise—especially after the events of Thursday night—she glanced his way with a fleeting smile that sent his heart lurching in his chest.

"Good point," Mr. Clements answered with a nod. "And there's no question that those Europeans were outright invaders in the Americas. There, the newcomers—or aliens, if you will—swarmed in without mercy, taking whatever they wanted, by force. They also brought waves of horrible disease that caught native peoples in the Western Hemisphere unprepared… something that I hope our leaders are bearing in mind right now."

Several students blanched at the idea. Mark recalled how

close he and his friends had been to the alien, breathing the same air! A plague from the stars. Now wouldn't that just round out the whole month?

"Elsewhere, things were more complicated. Especially for the first couple of centuries after da Gama's voyage, when Europeans came to Asia and Africa more as traders than conquerors, and where disease was much less of a factor. Even there, however, the arrival of a foreign culture and new technologies had profound effects, disrupting everything that had been static and assumed in local cultures. Even powerful nations that tried to control the effects of contact, like China and Japan, wound up destabilized, plunging into devastating internal strife.

"Still, none of those conflicts would match the bitter clash we've been studying for the last week, an awful conflagration that wracked Europe itself during the very same period."

This time, the groan from Dave and some others held a tone of grudging admiration for the smooth way the teacher segued discussion back into the syllabus. Mr. Clements swivelled toward a map that hung from the south wall, covered with arrows showing the harsh, back-and-forth struggle called the Sixty Years War.

"Can anyone explain why this period was even more riotous *inside* Europe than in far-off lands that their ships were surprising and exploiting?"

Trembling a little, Arlene Hsu raised her hand.

"B-because of the… Protestant Reformation?"

Mr. Clements always took a gentler tone when answering Arlene. It obviously took courage for her to speak up. Freewheeling class discussions hadn't been the style in school where she came from—a small town north of Shanghai.

"Yes, well, that was the reason given by kings and princes and city states for waging brutal war on their neighbors. A dispute over religious doctrine. But *does* that completely explain it? Anybody."

Forgetting his vow to stay silent, Mark raised a hand.

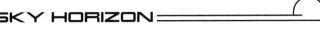

"Weren't they just as shook up by... by all this new *contact* with outsiders, as anybody else was?"

Mr. Clements smiled. Mark hoped it wasn't too obvious that the teacher felt grateful for being chosen as one of the Thursday night witnesses. He had clearly enjoyed the chance to participate, helping to transfer the alien into professional hands while also preventing any government cover-up... and getting to watch history happen in real-time.

Fine, but Mark didn't need 'teacher's pet' added to the things murmured behind his back.

"You may be onto something, Mr. Bamford. Their world *was* changing. Can anybody suggest what could have shaken up Europe, at this time?"

Hands raised. One student after another started contributing to a growing list.

"New weapons. New war tactics."

"All the gold stolen from Mexico. That would've changed the economy."

"There were new crops too... corn, potatoes, tobacco..."

"New *ideas*—"

"—spread by printing presses. Didn't all this happen just a little after that German guy, Gutberg—"

"Guttenberg."

"—yeah. Suddenly books and newspapers were cheap."

"And new ideas don't always bring folks together, do they? Sometimes they frighten people, or divide them. In the beginning, printing was more effective at spreading hate than encouraging tolerance. It took many generations to change that. Anything else?"

"How about dangerous ideas that came *from* those places the ships went?" Arlene asked, and Mr. Clements nodded.

"Interesting point, Arlene! Did cultural colonization go both ways, affecting the invaders as much as the invaded? That's not often talked about. Maybe you could do a paper."

Again, groans. Before the bell, several more research topics were sure to be assigned.

"How about—" Mark heard Helene say behind him, her voice more hushed than usual. "How about the very fact that the world was bigger... a much bigger place, after Columbus? Maybe that changed view kind of drove them all a bit... crazy?"

There was silence for several heartbeats after that, as each student let the implication sink in. How her words applied today. Even Mr. Clements appeared subdued.

Anyway, the point was made. Even Dave McCarty clearly realized it. History still had a place in the post-Contact world.

"Excellent, Helene. That would also make a really interesting topic for a—"

Mr. Clements halted when the door creaked open. A student carrying a hall pass entered, handing the teacher a slip of paper. He read it with a pursed brow.

"Bamford," he said at last, holding the slip out to Mark. "You're wanted in the main office."

Mark stood, lifting his backpack. He didn't dare look around to see how others took this—yet another sign of special treatment. But at least now he might escape new assignments.

"Check my web site," the teacher said as he departed, dashing even that silver lining. "Tonight's homework will be a thirty minute e-debate, at the usual time. You can take first chair in the argument *against* contact, Mark. We'll decide the exact topic while you're away."

Mark tried not to wince, especially with Helene watching. *I guess it wouldn't do for Clements to show gratitude, for my inviting him to help make history for a change, instead of just teaching it.*

The halls felt eerily empty with all students in class. Along with his footsteps, faint echoes carried indoors from the athletic field, where coaches hollered at the lazy as they had for generations. Mark shuffled along toward the administration suites, wondering *now what?*

There seemed little doubt that it must have to do with Xeno.

Sure enough, when he entered the main office Alex was already present. So was Barry Tang. They all shared a silent nod as the secretary ushered them into Principal Jeffers's office.

Jeffers cut an imposing figure. Almost two meters tall, he had actually trained for six weeks with the San Francisco Forty-Niners, before failing to make the final roster. That was many years ago, but he still kept the jersey from his brief pro career in a glass case, next to photos from his time as a Peace Corps volunteer. The principal believed that everyone should have a broad range of interests.

"Here they are," he said in a deep voice as the students came in. Two other adults turned at the same time, causing Mark to stumble briefly in surprise. One of them was an Air Force officer—his father!

The other, a pale-haired woman wearing a lab coat, smiled as Alex blurted—"Mom! What are you doing here?"

Dad shared a silent look with Mark, saying *wait and see.*

"We're still looking for Barry's folks," Principal Jeffers said. "I can't let him go on a field trip without their permission. So if you're really in a hurry..."

"We are, I'm afraid," Major Bamford said. "We'll just have to take Alex and Mark for now, and hope Barry can follow."

Alexandra blinked.

"Field trip?"

Mark's father drew a folded sheet of paper from his tunic pocket. It had official-looking seals and signatures—plus some odd-shaped blotchy symbols on the bottom.

"Not a normal one, by any means," he said. "It seems you've been invited."

"Invited?" This time it was Mark's turn express puzzlement.

"For a reunion. With the visitor. We're going to see your strange little man from the stars."

Special Assignments   3

Barry was devastated of course. He wheedled and complained. But nothing—no assurances about what his folks *would*
say—had any effect. Principal Jeffers was adamant. When it came
to responsibility for a minor, rules were rules. No signed permission slip? No exit from school grounds before the bell.

Driving them to the nearby base, Major Bamford seemed to
have added about four inches to his chest, all of it pride. As he commented to Dr. Behr, Alex's mother, "I've taken Mark around the
world with me. But now he's outdone all that in just a few days."

In other words, Dad knew that his own clearance and technical slot wouldn't normally let him anywhere near the alien. He
was getting in today solely as Mark's guardian and escort. Grin-
ning, he didn't seem to mind at all.

Dr. Behr, by contrast, was already part of a large team that
had been assembled to see to Xeno's needs. But she kept taciturn
about details. Though an international committee had been appointed to keep an eye on things, it remained mostly a U. S. government operation. Information would be released through channels in an 'orderly manner.'

A brief show of ID cards let them past the first checkpoint
onto the base. They drove by barracks, offices and the Post
Exchange before reaching a second guard post near the big
airfield. Here a second inspection was more rigorous. Each of
them had to get out of the car to face everything from dogs to

sophisticated scanners, while the vehicle itself got a thorough going-over. When that finished, they drove past the flight control tower and alongside a long runway. The howl of engines went bone-deep. A steady flow of fighters overhead escorted heavy transports as three of the heavier planes touched down, one after another. The caravan bore Mark and Alex toward a cluster of buildings that stood at the far end, offset from anything else, bordering only a vast expanse of desert, dotted with spiky Joshua trees.

A pair of old hangars had been hastily augmented with several white, inflatable structures. Dr. Behr explained that nearby trailers supplied air conditioning and environmental services. Vans came and went as Mark watched people in lab whites emerge through tunnels equipped with triple doors.

Airlocks, he realized, recalling how Mr. Clements had described the awful effects of 'alien' diseases on native populations, here on this very continent, just half a millennium ago.

Maybe I wasn't invited after all. Could this be just an excuse to get me into quarantine? Because I was exposed—

But that didn't make sense. The same thing could have been accomplished during the weekend. And he would have been quick to cooperate.

A lieutenant met them at the entrance to the biggest inflated structure, checking their identifications on an electronic clipboard. She accepted Mark's California driver's license, confirming its coded information, but then frowned over Alex's learner's permit—not exactly a *secure credential.* Well, anyone could tell she was barely sixteen. How much threat did they expect from a kid!

(Well, okay, a kid with a second-degree black belt, who could scurry up a rock wall like a spider.)

Finally, something flashed on the lieutenant's smart clipboard and she stepped aside. "Please suit up. Coveralls and booties. Don't put on gloves or masks unless you're asked to by your guide."

Dr. Behr smiled and explained as they entered.

"We're still taking precautions, though by now we're pretty sure the chance of cross-infection is minimal."

Deeply relieved, Mark passed through a sealed pathway. It felt like walking in a long, slender bubble. Their group passed two more sets of hissing irises before entering a large chamber where slick-textured dungarees hung from hooks along one wall. Dr. Behr helped them put on slipperlike shoe-covers and snug caps, leaving only their hands and faces exposed.

"We have a filtered laminar airflow system. Nobody wears masks anymore unless they get real close. It looks as if the Garubis' microbial parasites don't have a clue how to attack Earthling body cells, and vice versa."

"Garubis?"

Dr. Behr glanced at Mark.

"Oh, that's right. You haven't heard. It's all coming out in a press conference, this evening. The news couldn't be more exciting." She smiled and suddenly Mark glimpsed what Alex might look like, when she grew up a little more. If her luck held.

"First, we know their species name. They are called *Garubis.* And there's more. Helped by a worldwide network of experts with high-speed computers... and some gifted amateurs who joined in via the web... we've managed to crack the language barrier!"

"So fast!" Alex said, beaming at her mother. "That seems impossible."

"He helped us." Dr. Behr gestured ahead of them, toward the next enclosure they were now appeoaching. "In fact, that's why you two kids were invited here today."

"Um," Mark nodded. "Invited?"

The word still sounded improbable.

"That's right. It was almost the first thing Na-bistaka asked for, once we started talking. He wanted to see the kids who rescued him."

It was almost too much to take in at once. *Na-bistaka,* the xeno's name. And the word—'rescued'.

Mark suddenly realized that a knot of tension had been coiled inside of him for days, worrying about that. *Had* he and Alex really done the right thing? No matter what was said by the students at TNPHS—or adults, or the news media or government officials—only one entity had the right to decide.

He understood part of the reason when they rounded the next corner and saw the alien's new accommodations.

Good-bye kennel cage, hello Plaza Hotel!

Well, that might overstate the difference. It was still an enclosure and the 'visitor' wasn't exactly free to depart and enjoy every nearby tourist spot. But the glass panels had curtains on the inside, which evidently could be closed whenever the occupant chose.

Within, a kind of *nest* had been created on top of a four-poster bed, using strips of fabric. Nearby, some small tables and chairs must have come from a childrens furniture store. Mark spotted a refrigerator, a microwave oven and a food processor, arrayed in a half-sized kitchenette… plus a stainless steel bucket with a spring lid that had sticky, grayish-red dribbles down one side. He shuddered, knowing what that was for.

This strange creature can cross the gulf of stars. But doesn't bother to maintain cleanliness in its own living space?

An entire wall was made up of top quality audio-visual and computer equipment—six or seven giant flat-screens—while a trestle table lay strewn with all kinds of objects, from books to dolls to construction toys. Three humans stood near a second table wearing gauze masks, but these had been pulled down to let them speak more freely. One fellow tapped excitedly on a big display that showed bright pinpoints, annotated with letters and numbers.

A star chart, Mark realized. Another person huddled over some kind of technical schematic, shaking her head.

All of that was peripheral, of course. The center of attention could only be a short figure on the left, standing next to the second scientist, wearing a hooded silk bathrobe—bright scarlet— that dragged on the floor, preventing any view of the wearer's body. Mark did hear a voice, though—the same *chuttering* sound

that he remembered from that brief encounter in Larry Gornet's cabaña.

Soon, an amplified computer translation echoed from nearby speakers.

"No. No. No. Your electronic devices will not deliver the degrees of modulation necessary to create a quantum tunnelling effect. It appears that I shall have to draw upon yet another of my precious emergency storage units, in order to recall the design parameters and draw them for you."

The computer-generated translation conveyed a tone of resignation, plus something else. Was Mark just imagining *disdain* in the flat, toneless words?

"Wow," commented Alexandra.

Her mother agreed with an emphatic nod. "Wow is right! I've been away just a few hours, and yet the level of syntactical abstraction has improved remarkably, along with grammatical construction. Those self-correcting language algorithms from Carnegie are just fantastic!"

Alex shook her head.

"No, I mean wow... he's teaching us how to make a machine that can do *quantum tunnelling?* I thought that was just in Star Trek."

Then she blinked a couple of times and glanced at Mark, who nodded back.

We are in Star Trek. Or something scarier.

"What's the objective?" Major Bamford asked, standing on his toes to peer at the schematics. If they were secret, they had no business being out in the open like this. "What are you trying to build?"

Not a spacecraft or transport, Mark realized. The design looked way too simple, no fuselage or flight surfaces. No place for a passenger. Anyway, he doubted that *Na-bistaka* needed something like that right now.

"A radio," he guessed.

Dr. Behr nodded. "That's right, Mark. Just as soon as we

could talk to each other, Na-bistaka started teaching us how to help him to... well... phone home."

She shrugged at using such an obvious cliche. And for a moment there seemed little to say. Not until Major Bamford asked.

"Are we going to do that? Yell for his friends to come get him?"

"Good question. It's a matter for debate... for the whole world to discuss. And after tonight, the discussion will be wide open. Nobody should be excluded.

"Obviously, there are ramifications. Right now, there's still a chance to limit this contact—though at some moral cost. But once we've sent Na-bistaka's message..."

She let the implications hang.

Once we've sent it, everything that we talked about this morning in Mr. Clement's class will begin, Mark knew. *We'll enter a time of struggle and change. One in which we're the primitives, underdogs, struggling to catch up.*

Even if the aliens are as nice as can be... there will be challenges and pain. More than any of us can imagine.

Mark couldn't help feeling a little guilty about that.

He thought about those native Mexican tribes who allied themselves with Hernan Cortez, helping him conquer the hated Aztecs. Would those allies have treated the Spaniards so well, if they had an inkling what might come next?

Should we help this creature? Or hide him somewhere and hope his friends never show up to ask about him? Maybe Scott's plan would have been better after all... a brief celebrity curiosity, that then vanished into legend.

Mark felt guilty for thinking that, too.

"So, do we get anything in exchange for helping?" Major Bamford asked. Dad was always the pragmatist—the eternal optimist—of the family.

"Good question. We're studying the capsule he arrived in. It seems to be just a life raft, lacking any of the really juicy technologies for interstellar flight. Still, the circuits and things he's teaching us to build for the communication device may help us understand some key principles. As for any formal *quid pro quo?* We haven't raised the issue of trade or compensation. It seemed… premature."

Mark wondered what he would ask for, if the occasion ever came up. Then he realized, it might be very close. *What'll I say, if he suddenly offers me three wishes?*

Yeah, a dumb thought. But he found that his brain wasn't working too well. In fact, it felt like mush.

The scarlet dressing gown abruptly straightened, rising a little taller, as if the wearer sensed something. The hooded figure turned slowly, until a pair of gleaming, golden eyes appeared, set weirdly on both sides of a slender snout. The alien face—even more unnerving than it had been in poor lighting—seemed to change as its gaze settled on Mark and Alex. Somehow, it conveyed recognition.

He knows us.

Abandoning the technician and schematics, Na-bistaka moved closer, facing the glass partition and dropping onto a pile of cushions. One gnarly hand lifted, raising a floppy sleeve, to point at Mark and his friend. More chuttering sounds emerged.

"You came." said a wall speaker, conveying the computer translation. *"In studying your primitive data stores, I found it culturally problematic whether larval humans would be allowed to attend me, even at my direct request. Does this mean you have advanced? Have you been promoted, because of your actions, to adult status?"*

Mark blinked. He glanced at Alex, recalling her learner's permit, and thought about his own steep car insurance rates. And poor Barry, who could not come at all, because of the school district's absurdly overprotective rules.

"Um… I don't think so. We're here with our parents."

The golden eyes rotated independently—an eerie sight—to examine Major Bamford and Dr. Behr.

"Superintended contact with an outsider. Consistent with low

reproductive rates and high nurturing emphasis. Yet, from direct experience I know that the late-larval form is allowed to form undisciplined and unsupervised cultural association units.

"Moreover, these pseudo-tribal units may freely conspire against the interests of the common good! Is this a common pattern?"

This time, Mark had to think hard. Na-bistaka was talking about high school, about the cliques that form among teens… and about how some of them recently got carried away with their own sense of drama and rebellion, attempting to handle a major event—one with implications for all humanity—completely by themselves.

"It happens," Alex answered. "Kids today have more freedom to experiment. Maybe too much. Or too little. There's a lot of arguments."

The alien castaway's snout opened and closed a few times.

"Argument seems endemic to the peculiar culture that produces the most noise on this planet. One that is rife with mutual suspicion and recrimination. Disorganization and abandonment of tradition. These things I attempted to study from afar, before the malfunction."

Mark squelched a temptation to feel insulted. After all, Na-bistaka wasn't saying anything new about contemporary American life. The *noise* he must have been analyzing from some cloaked perch in space, came from Earth's electronic media. The 'malfunction' was presumably what led to him become stranded in the California desert, to be picked up by undisciplined larval humans.

"Well," Mark answered. "I'm glad things turned out all right."

That brought a strange sound from the creature within the enclosure.

"Have they?"

Mark blinked. "What?"

"Have they turned out all right?"

Somehow, the computerized translation sounded bemused by the question.

"Certainly my own position was improved by your intervention, transferring my custody to more responsible parties. You personally acted to divert destiny onto a fresh path, one with unforeseen future outcomes."

Mark wasn't sure he liked the sound of that. Na-bistaka's statement had an ominous quality. He swallowed, unable to think what to say.

"What do you mean?" Alexandra asked, stepping forward to the glass that separated her from the alien.

"I mean that there will now be consequences. All actions have them.

"Are you prepared to reap what you have sown?"

Open Discussion 4

The planet called Earth launched into its first-ever universal conversation.

At one level or another, a majority of the eight billion inhabitants took part—some through electronic forums and scientifically tabulated opinion polls, while countless others participated through the babble of rumor and argument in teahouses, marketplaces and teeming bazaars. News and debate trickled down via mass media while public perceptions percolated upward, even in dictatorships. Local officials asked hairdressers, taxi drivers and bartenders what people were saying, then passed word to mayors, then governors and so on.

The Great Discussion was ardent. Opinionated. Boulevards filled with mass demonstrations. Here and there, fevered emotions broke into riots. Some buildings and effigies burned...

... and yet, for the most part—to the surprise of nearly everyone—the debate was rather earnest. This issue seemed to go beyond nationalism or politics. It was just too important for most people to leave to passion.

Shall we transmit a message?

That was the central question, solemnly argued from back alleys in Dacca to the yacht basins of Sydney, from impoverished hovels in Quito, where the TV was the only source of illumination, to penthouse apartments in Montevideo.

Shall we send the xeno-guest's call for help?

If it were simply a matter of beaming a radio bulletin to space, there would be no point even raising the issue. All sorts of nations, cities and even private individuals owned high-poewer transmitters. Even if the world reached a 99% agreement to stay quiet, *somebody* would surely disagree and defy mass opinion by shouting to the stars. Today, more than ever, it was the human way.

But it seemed that new and sophisticated technologies were needed, in order to send an SOS bulletin to the nearest Garubis outpost. For now and the immediate future, only the U.S. government had a clue how to build such machinery.

In theory, the United Nations Supervisory Committee could insist that those blueprints be posted on the internet. But they had no intention of doing that. Perhaps not ever.

It all hung on what the *world consensus* decided—if agreement proved possible at all. For weeks, it did not seem to be.

Meanwhile, for Mark Bamford, it was back to the grind. Back to high school—the modern form of incarceration for those found guilty of being young.

In some other era, a sturdy fellow who had just turned seventeen might be a confident hunter, already at the top of his skill, faster and more daring than anyone else in the band. As a farmer, he would have fields to plow and probably a family to feed. In ancient kingdoms like Rome or Babylon, a seventeen year old might by now have scars from a soldier's battles. And he would know how to make nearly all of his own tools.

Even until a few decades ago, if you were *really* desperate to escape high school, you could always drop out and enlist.

No longer. Nowadays, even the army wouldn't take you without a diploma. So, you might as well just stick it out, get grades, go to college. Sure, nobody would take you seriously *there*, either; but at least college was more interesting and fun. You'd finally get an adult's freedom—without the responsibilities… or any of the respect.

Till graduation, then, life was on hold however you looked at it. Just one thought made the prospect bearable.

Everybody has to go through this.

It's just my turn.

Only now that wasn't exactly true, was it? The news cameras had vanished from Twenty Nine Palms High within a week after that fateful Thursday. Yet, so long as the whole world was transfixed on the issue of first contact, Mark's position at school settled into a rhythm of grinding discomfort.

It wasn't all sullen silence. In fact, a few more students spoke to him than before all this started; though most seemed interested in latching-on somehow. Perhaps out of some vain hope of being invited to meet the Xeno. Few of them stayed interested after they realized the truth. He lacked any special back door pass. That one encounter at the base had been pretty much it.

Even Gornet's pals stopped following him around with *horking* sounds. They still glowered, and Mark felt certain they would have pounced by now, pummelling him after school—except that it seemed pointless.

I have a reputation as a tattler, he realized. *They won't beat me up because they think I'd squeal.*

He wouldn't! Not over a simple bruising. He wanted to tell them that. Get it over with, dammit! The guerrillitas near Caracas had been far more frightening than any gang of SoCal athletes. Anyway, they might be surprised at how many licks he'd get in.

But he kept his mouth shut. Anything Mark said now would just be used for mockery.

He stopped using his locker. Every time Alex and Frank Mills accompanied him to practice at the climbing wall, Mark carefully checked the ropes. Once, he found a few suspicious nicks, which he repaired without comment.

Beyond that, the goal was to endure till summer. *Just one more year,* he told himself.

Banners announced the theme for this year's Homecoming

Festival. Mark winced at the alien motif—silvery UFO types, still more popular in the public mind than the weirdly realistic Garubis image. There was even talk of changing the school mascot from a cartoony spy to E.T.

Agh, he thought, wishing Dad would just get promoted or transferred again. But as the crank callers and drive-by vandals went away, Major Bamford returned to his squadron, now in the thick of testing new "gimmicks" using bits of alien technology. In fact, Mark hadn't seen Dad so happy since before Mom died.

I might be too, if I had something useful to do.

Even history class was no escape. Mr. Clements finally gave up trying to focus on the past. Now, every discussion had something to do with the great big international debate over The Message.

Today's class focused on the surprise announcement by an ecumenical conclave of religious leaders, ranging from the Pope and Dalai Lama to Jewish, Muslim and Hindu scholars.

Morally, we must transmit the Visitor's call for help, stated the joint declaration. *Whether these beings prove beneficent or hostile, it is vital that we begin relations with a righteous act. We must, all of us together, put our trust in God.*

This communiqué had profound effects worldwide, even on non-believers. Never before had a single choice been portrayed in the same moral terms by all major faiths at the same time. Some of Mark's fellow students were also influenced to change their minds. But not Dave McCarty.

"It's all propaganda," he muttered. "The priests have had the masses in their grip for centuries. Since before there was writing! Now they're doing it again."

Arlene Hsu shook her head. She had grown more confident during the last two months, exchanging ideas informally and with increasing boldness, in the American style.

"How can you say they are insincere, Dave! Contact with a huge and powerful alien culture will bring in new ideas, challenging all of the old faiths. Why should the religious leaders *want* competition—"

"Because they're confident they'll win out, of course. I bet they see a chance to grab converts among the stars! Or maybe they just believe their own propaganda."

Mr. Clements stepped around to sit on the front of his desk.

"You use that word pretty freely, Dave. Do you have a clear idea what it means?"

"What? *Propaganda?*" McCarty blinked a couple of times. It was one of those terms you just grew up using, without ever seeing it defined.

"Propaganda... is where the folks with power or money or influence—"

"—elites—"

"Yeah, elites want the masses to believe something that'll help keep em under control, doing what the masters want. In olden times they did it by preaching *'obey the kings and priests.'* They did it in temples and churches and when they hired guys like Homer to chant songs about heroes and gods..."

"And nowadays they do it with television, movies, commercials." Hodge Takahashi interrupted, with a nod to his friend.

"...and *schools.*" Dave finished. That triggered agreeing laughter from several students.

"So," Mr. Clements concluded, tapping his own chest. "That makes me a tool of the establishment, cramming conformity messages into the minds of the young, molding them into obedient, compliant little villagers."

"And consumers!" interjected Paulina Isfahani. "Got to keep the economy churning, after all."

The teacher sighed. "Ah, it's sad. You're all too young to be so cynical."

That won him a flurry of groans that he tolerated with a grin.

"And yet, I wonder—could that be a clue?"

The remark drew puzzled looks.

"You mean the fact *that* we're cynical?" asked Helene Shockley from behind Mark. He didn't have to turn around; Mark knew exactly what she was wearing today—a turquoise top with beaded trim and a plunging neckline that stopped just short of breaking the school's liberal dress code.

"A clue to what, Mr. Clements?" Helene finished.

"Why, a clue to *which* propaganda messages we should be watching out for, of course. You all seem to agree that indoctrination fills the airwaves, newspapers, movies—and the schools," he conceded with a nod to Dave. "Persuasive messages that are nevertheless too subtle to be noticed by the common man or woman on the street. Right?"

Nods of agreement all around.

"But *you* are all capable of noticing, and rising above, this pervasive brainwashing. Is that it?"

More nods, though not quite as quick or vigorous as before. *Uh-oh,* Mark thought, sensing one of the teacher's trademark logical traps.

"How fortunate I am that you seventeen-year-old juniors in *my* history class happen to be so much smarter and more observant than all those sheep out there! All the doctors and lawyers and mechanics and such—*they* can't resist the brainwashing, but you have. How do you account for this amazing statistical fluke? Anybody?"

Now there was stone silence, till Arlene raised her hand again.

"Everybody likes to think *they* are smart, I guess… and that everyone else is clueless."

Mr. Clements nodded. "Some of you, at university, will take a class in the scientific method and learn how easily we are fooled by what we *want* to believe. You'll be sent out to survey people on the street, asking two questions. *How did you arrive at your own set of beliefs? And why do your opponents believe what they do?*

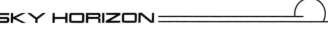

"Can anyone guess what nearly always happens?"

"Um… isn't it obvious?" Mark ventured. "People say they got their *own* beliefs by looking at the evidence."

"Right." The teacher pointed at him. "And this crosses all boundaries of politics or culture. Left or right or whatever. We ascribe our own opinions to *logical appraisal of the situation*, while we think that our enemies believe what they do because of *flaws in their character*."

Helene mulled this over, then commented.

"I guess that's human nature. We come up with reasons to think well of ourselves, and put down those we don't like. It makes their opinions seem less important. Especially when they don't like us."

This time, Mark turned around in time to catch Helene looking briefly at him! Her expression, friendly—and perhaps more— made him swivel forward again, awash in confusion. Was there some kind of double meaning in her words?

Paulina jumped in.

"Are you suggesting *we* may be as brainwashed as anybody else? But you said we're cynical!" She shook her head. "Unless… unless *that's* the clue you were talking about."

"Could be," Mr. Clements said. "But first, what do you consider to be the principal propaganda message of our time? Come on, let's have it. Something really extensive and widespread, that we swim through every day."

Hodge spoke up first.

"Commercialism! Be a good consumer. Buy stuff!"

"Hmm, yes. By volume—in the sheer number of messages— advertising can't be beat. But look at how thick-skinned the average person is toward commercials! I remember some old sci-fi novels predicted that people would march like morons to buy whatever they were told to. But reality is different. Every year advertisers struggle harder to amuse us, spending millions for a little name recognition. Nope. Try again."

"Religion," Dave said, succinctly, with his arms crossed and jaw set. That drew objections from Karen, Tasha and Jerome, who called Dave *intolerant.*

"The most paramount theme is conformity," suggested Arlene. "From an early age... in China...." Then she paused, suddenly unable to continue.

The teacher nodded. "It may surprise you to hear that I agree. Conformity is a potent theme that drives every society—at least every one I've heard of. Powerful forces push individuals to please their neighbors, and especially their tribal elites. At your age it's oversimplified with the term *peer pressure.* Some of it obviously comes from self-interest—it helps to have friends...."

Ouch, Mark thought. He still felt confused by that look from Helene, a moment ago. Had there been some kind of under-meaning, for him alone?

"...And yes, most societies actively preached conformity. Citizens were urged to resist disapproved influences and toe the line. This kind of indoctrination was common, in law and myth.

"But universal? Might *our* society be an exception?"

Mr. Clements paused.

"Can any of you name a recent movie that actively preached conformity? 'Be like everybody else and suppress your individuality'? How about any rock videos or popular novels? Can you come up with a single example? Even *one* in which the hero seemed to say that everybody should be the same?"

This time, silence stretched for half a minute.

Slowly, as if it might be a mistake, Mark lifted his hand.

"I think the message in movies... is nearly always the opposite."

"What do you mean?"

"Well, doesn't the hero, most of the time, kind of *stick it* to some evil rich guy? Or some government agency?"

"Or powerful criminals, or some other nasty elite." Mr. Clements nodded. "Usually, it starts in the first ten minutes of a film. There

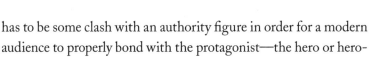

has to be some clash with an authority figure in order for a modern audience to properly bond with the protagonist—the hero or hero-ine. Even if it's just a snide remark, mumbled about the boss or a neighborhood bigshot. Can anyone think of an exception?"

Mark could see his classmates wracking their brains. Especially Dave and Hodge, who clearly didn't like where this was heading.

"Suspicion of authority," the teacher said. "That's the theme filling our media tales, novels and videos. The main character has to display some quirk of individualism, some underdog eccentricity or independent streak, even if she starts out as an aristocrat or princess. Often it doesn't matter *which* authority figure gets defied. If the writer or director is politically right-of-center, it may be government or intellectuals. If she's more to the left, it could be a faceless, inhumane *corporation.* Or vicious drug lords, or some foreign power… or maybe a threat from outer space."

He wrote on the chalkboard. "One of your assignments will be to get examples. Tally how many modern films you can find that preach suspicion of authority, and its companion message—*tolerance* of eccentricity.

"For comparison, also list films or videos, *if any,* that push the opposite message—conformity and/or intolerance."

"But—" Dave McCarty sputtered. "How could suspicion of authority be propaganda! Are you suggesting that some conspiracy of secret masters one day decided—'Hey, let's start a campaign so people will hate conspiracies and secret masters?' Is that it?"

"Calm down, Dave. And no, I'm not saying it was planned… though it might be an idea worth chewing on." He smiled. "I figure we've been doing it ourselves, subconsciously, by paying to see entertainments that reinforce something we—"

"—already believe," Karen blurted, then rushed on to object. "But then why hasn't anybody noticed!"

"*I* noticed." Arlene Hsu raised her hand again. Some of the old shyness returned to her voice. "We *all* noticed, back in Shantung. American movie heroes… never show respect."

From behind him, Mark heard Helene Shockley respond. "I think maybe *we* don't notice because it's hard to—"

"—notice propaganda that you already agree with," Mark found himself finishing for her. He glanced at Helene apologetically, then away again quickly. There had been another friendly, enigmatic smile.

Now Dave McCarty was really angry. "You're saying we're *taught* to be individualists? That society *wants* us to defy authority? That—"

"That *you* didn't invent it, Dave?" murmured Paulina. "Any more than you invented the black leather look." She pointed at his studded jacket. "Yeah, I can live with that."

Not if looks could kill, Mark thought, as poor Dave glared at her. A strangled noise gurgled, but before Dave could gather words, the class period bell rang.

"Check my web site for the full assignment!" Mr. Clements called to those rushing for the door. Half a dozen students gathered near his desk to continue arguing till the last possible moment. It illustrated why Mark had invited the teacher to be a witness, that crazy Thursday night (it felt like a lifetime ago). In Mr. Clements' Class, you almost felt like you were in college, instead of just a great big warehouse for teens.

Mark wasn't one of those lingering behind. He hurried outside and turned to wait as throngs of students pushed past him in the hall. When Helene emerged, would there be something in her eyes again? If so, should he speak? What could he say?

Here she comes, he thought—

—only to be shouldered aside as someone much taller forged past. It wasn't a violent or aggressive shove. The rangy boy even muttered a friendly, reflex apology. No big deal; you got used to being jostled in the halls. And yet….

Scott Tepper grinned, taking Helene's elbow as she emerged. The senior whispered in her ear and she laughed, shaking the coiled black ringlets of her hair. As they turned to head off together, Helene did offer Mark another glancing smile—it was friendly.

But that's all. Friendly. He must have imagined anything else.

He felt like a robot through Algebra and English. In Chemistry, Alexandra tried to snap him out of it by threatening to set fire to his sleeve with the bunsen burner. She and Barry Tang—it was the one class they all took together—had to take care of the rest of their joint experiment without Mark's inept assistance.

What finally broke his spell of self-pity, a little while later, was a sudden news flash that rocked the lunch court, sending everybody diving into their backpacks for their cell phones, radios and palm-links.

There had been an assassination attempt—an attack against the Contact Center—at the air base just outside of town.

Announcements (5)

"There are still people who feel desperate to stop a Message from going out," Major Bamford explained that night, between gulps of reheated stew. "Seeing the shift in public opinion, they decided to act first."

Mark found it hard to believe his father could be so calm after today's near disaster. His own gut still churned over televised scenes showing wreckage from *eight* remote-controlled aircraft that had tried to swoop down from every direction at once, outfitted with basic stealth technology and piloted close to ground till the very last moment. All of which suggested sophisticated technical backing and high levels of funding. One of the drones, filled with high explosives, even managed to strike a building next to the Contact Center—a hangar where hybrid aircraft were being tested with morsels of alien technology.

Dad works there.

That had been his sole thought while watching images of the smashed, burning facility. Ambulances came and went—he could hear them in the distance when he stepped outside. On TV their strobe lights diffracted through clots of roiling smoke onto charred bodies. For a while Mark feared the worst, for his father and for the guest from the stars.

Then word came. Na-bistaka had remained safe the whole time, under those inflated domes. And Major Bamford sent a hurried message, telling Mark to go ahead and have dinner without him.

Then, much later over midnight cocoa, the tired Air Force officer described today's momentous attack as only a close eye-witness could—starting with the sudden wail of alert sirens, followed by a *crump* and *hiss* of departing anti-aircraft missiles, then the brittle hum of close-in defense lasers—and finally a series of deafening explosions.

The main habitat suffered no damage. The visitor-guest, Na-bistaka, wasn't harmed—but it had been an awfully near thing. And even though the assault failed in its main goal, there were casualties. Dad's squadron lost a couple of colleagues. Working deep inside one of the experimental jets, they had been unable to take cover in time. Hours later, he was obviously angry about that, but also strangely composed—almost serene.

It's how you're supposed to act, in a crisis, Mark thought, wishing he were made of the same stuff.

"I can take comfort in one thing," his father said. "The bastards have already lost."

That was the latest news, announced even as Major Bamford drove home for a late supper. The assassination attempt had only served to consolidate world opinion. Shortly afterward, the International Contact Conference on the island of Malta took its long-delayed vote, achieving that most remarkable accomplishment—*consensus.*

Planet Earth's human civilization, acting in unison, would help a stranded castaway from the stars.

The Message would go forth.

And immediately. So that no one else could see murder as a viable alternative.

Like it or not, for better or for worse, humanity was committed.

"So… what do you think will happen now, Dad?"

Mark's father smiled. The corners of his eyes creased near streaks of gray.

"Who can say? I know just one thing for sure, son—the world you'll live in will be different than the one my generation knew.

We better hope that we succeeded in raising you kids well—to have agile minds and resilient souls. Because it's a sure thing you'll need both."

Staying up till the wee hours, they watched televised coverage as workers prepared to cast forth *The Message,* from an antenna that had been prepared a few hundred miles away, in an isolated Nevada valley. The moment that the switch was pulled, Mark felt a sudden tightness in his throat. Did the abrupt sensation come from some side effect of *quantum tunnelling* when the signal burst forth? Did everyone on Earth feel the same thing, at the very same instant? Or was it a psychological thing—a symptom of realizing at last.

That's it. No turning back.

One thing he sure didn't expect... and he doubted that anyone else did either.

He never imagined the Garubis would reply so soon.

Honored Guests 6

A rescue ship arrived just ten days after the Message was sent.

It entered orbit three hundred miles up—a giant cylinder that rolled swiftly around its long axis. Mirrorlike, it reflected the glitter of starlight, and vastly dwarfed the International Space Station.

Communications from the star-galleon were brusque at first, consisting of a simple statement in the Garubis tongue, demanding to speak with Na-bistaka. When that connection was made, linking directly to the alien's habitat near Twenty-Nine Palms, a whirl of chuttering conversation ensued, so rapid that it taxed the new translation programs. However, one exchange came through perfectly clear.

How did the natives treat you?

The world waited tensely, then sighed in relief at Na-bistaka's reply.

After some initial discomfort... better than expected.

What followed seemed harder to decipher. One expert thought there was a tone of disappointment in the starship's reply. Something that might be translated as—*too bad.* Other linguists dismissed this guess as pure imagination. After all, how could such a reaction even make sense?

Anyway, public attention soon shifted to a brief spat between the U.S. State Department and the U.N. Contact Commission, bickering over where to invite the Garubis to land. They finally agreed that, even though the Americans had proved worthy of continuing their leading role, Washington D.C. was too much of a national symbol. And the California desert was too isolated.

When the visitors affirmed that they could touch down a lander with high accuracy and only slight disruption, a bold but popular decision was reached.

In forty-eight hours the Garubis would bring their rescue vehicle to Unity Park, on lower Manhattan Island, in the City of New York.

It happened on a Saturday, so they made a party of the event in the Bamford living room. Dad worked at the kitchen table, poring over recent photos taken of the orbiting spacecraft, while Mark and his friends scarfed popcorn and cokes in front of a media array featuring several borrowed flat screen sets and web-links.

Twenty-Nine Palms seemed a ghost town. Pizza delivery places were the only businesses at work, and they had a three hour backlog. Even the swarm of TV vans that had staked-out the nearby air base for months finally dispersed that morning, when Na-bistaka's plane departed under escort by a squadron of USAF fighters. For a while, reporters prowled the desert community like hungry wolves, stopping occasionally by the Bamford house in hope of a bite. Mark never emerged. Alex and Barry had avoided the reporters by the simple expedience of sneaking in the back way, parking their bikes in the alley and then vaulting over the Fortinis' back fence. (Well, Alex vaulted. Barry grunted and slithered.)

Anyway, it seemed logical to meet here. Alex's parents were out of town, having gone ahead to help prepare the way for Na-bistaka in New York. And the Tang family, for some reason that Mark never fathomed, did not own a TV.

So they settled in to watch, by web and cable and satellite dish, as history was being made.

But not for a while. At first, all the fancy modern gear carried was nothing but wave after wave of *talk*. Conjecture and groundless speculation. What kind of law reigned out there on the vast star-lanes? Was there a Galactic Federation of some sort? Nabistaka had affirmed that the Garubis weren't alone out there. He even mentioned a few species names and sketched a few strange faces... then stopped providing any further information, saying that such things weren't in his area of expertise.

We never did find out what his job really is, Mark pondered. *Or why he came all this way to Earth.* The xeno-visitor was very good at keeping things close to the chest.

"Well, after all," one pundit ventured. "If *you* were accidentally thrown into a first contact situation, wouldn't you find it wise to keep quiet, till specialists could be called in? To do otherwise might be irresponsible!" The expert blabbed on that way for quite some time, apparently unaware of any irony.

While professional talkers kept the waiting world distracted, New York prepared, once again, to take center stage as World Party Headquarters. Bridges and tunnels groaned as crowds of the timid left town, perhaps with terrifying sci fi movie scenarios in mind...

... and replacement throngs poured *in*, eager to help celebrate the dawn of a new era. Clearly, it was a matter of temperament, and humanity had all kinds. A variety that had only been enhanced by a culture that preached a love of individual eccentricity.

"Diversity is strength," commented one of the onscreen pundits. But Mark recalled something else that his biology teacher had said, a year ago.

Diversity is the grist of evolution.

Berthed at the waterfront next to Unity Park, two giant cruise liners were being frantically readied to host visiting star-emissaries, in case they wanted more room than a mere landing craft could provide. Liners seemed ideal because they were already relatively self-contained, almost like a spaceship, even down to storing waste products aboard sealed tanks. Anything the visitors found distasteful could be removed and whatever they liked could be swiftly brought aboard. Barges were already rushing in every kind of food that Na-bistaka found pleasant during his stay.

Meanwhile, on Manhattan's East Side a short mile away crosstown, the United Nations dropped all other business as presidents, royalty and other top dignitaries arrived to take part in the most important meeting ever. No plans had been discussed with the Garubis so far, but it was assumed that their ambassador or emissary would want to address world leaders.

Nor were 'just people' to be left out. Along vacated First Avenue, a series of giant canopies served the world's raucous special interest groups—from environmental and religious associations to industrial and labor organizations. From scientific academies to bickering ethnicities. Huge banners spread open, offering greetings in many tongues, or else appealing for miraculous intervention. Everybody, it seemed, who perceived a special problem aching to be solved, sent envoys. And the Big Apple stretched to accommodate them all.

Leave nobody out, that seemed to be the motto. No one commented or seemed to notice that the scene ran counter to every old-fashioned science fiction scenario, cliches that were nearly always cynically based on notions of universal panic, or secrecy.

This belongs to everyone.

Yes, that sounded like an impossible ideal. Welcoming honored guests. Keeping them safe. Handling a million sober details and preparing for ten times as many contingencies. Listening to all concerns... while giving free rein to a natural wish to celebrate. Sure, it was impossible. But if any city could manage, this one could.

Besides, who knew yet which of humanity's nagging troubles might be solved by Contact? Some enthusiasts were bound to be disappointed while others might have their wildest dreams come true. Immortality? Warp drive? Teleportation? Realistic 'holo-decks' that offered experience better than real life?

Wiser heads were cautioning against fevered expectation. Some problems might not have easy answers. Others could fall into the disappointing category of 'later, when you're ready.'

"They may be almost as confused by us as we are by them," mused one sage on a news program. "We can't assume, for ex-ample, that they'll give us a magic formula for world peace. We've been slowly learning *how* to do that all by ourselves, for several generations. What we've lacked so far has been the will."

Others disagreed.

"Imagine asking the Garubis to serve as neutral *arbitrators,*" a competing commentator gushed. "They would have nothing to gain by one side winning unfairly over another. We could settle so many ancient disputes—Palestine, Kashmir, Korea, the Sudan—simply by agreeing in advance to accept a fair, impartial judge-ment that gives something to everybody!"

The ensuing argument grew so heated that Mark changed channels.

Scientists appeared to be more interested in what could be learned from an advanced, starfaring civilization about nature's laws.

"Naturally, I have mixed feelings," said one Nobel Prize winner. "I spent my whole life becoming a top expert in my field. Here on Earth and—so far as we once knew—in the whole universe."

He laughed. "Now I must go back to school. Elementary school, perhaps!"

Mark noted that the graying researcher didn't look all that chagrined by the prospect of losing his 'expert' status, or even returning to basics. In fact, it seemed to delight him. *Some people are just wiser and more flexible than I'll ever be,* he thought with a sigh.

On one thing every commentator seemed to agree. "We ought to know by now, if the Garubis were outright hostile," one of them summed-up. At worst, the universe was about to open up to humanity. Maybe a lot.

"We may soon have new tools, helping us become a whole lot richer," one historian said, then arched her eyebrow. "While at the same time making us *feel* much poorer, in comparison to others out there. Keeping some perspective may be crucial. Let's learn from the mistakes made by *both* sides during past episodes of first contact—between Earthling cultures a few centuries ago. We must be bold and dynamic, while at the same time keeping our feet firmly planted in reality. On Mother Earth."

Around two in the afternoon, even as Na-bistaka's plane arrived at Newark Airport, amateur astronomers reported visually sighting the Lander. A *disk* had peeled off one end of the great, orbiting starship and was now dropping through Earth's atmosphere like a frisbee, spinning as it threw off gouts of friction heat.

"Dang, it's big!" Barry said as reports poured in from along the vessel's glide path. "Maybe five city blocks."

Mark glanced at the cleared area in Unity Park, surrounded by National Guard troops facing outward to keep back the crowds. *Some trees may not survive,* he guessed, though still there should be enough room.

After making sure his friends had all they needed, Mark went to check on Dad, who still sat at the kitchen table, poring over photographs and charts. Officially, nothing was supposed to be top secret about this interstellar contact. Still it surprised Mark that his father had brought this material home for the weekend.

On one side were pictures taken by orbital satellites, of the gleaming Garubis star galleon. To the right were images of a much smaller craft—the lifeboat that brought Na-bistaka down to the Southern California desert for his initial encounter with "human larval forms" in their strange high school tribes.

Major Bamford tapped a photo taken after the escape capsule had been unburied by an Air Force recovery team. "This still puzzles me," he told Mark.

"What does?"

Dad shook his head. "What doesn't? We never learned what 'malfunction' forced Na-bistaka to make an emergency landing... or indeed, what happened to his ship. Was it completely destroyed? Is it stranded on the far side of the moon?"

"Maybe we'll find out when his people go salvage it," Mark suggested. Then he added with a grin. "I bet *you* hope it's abandoned. Left behind as scrap. Then you might get sent to look it over?"

They had discussed this, of course. Dad was no astronaut, but soon there might be so much to do in space—so many urgent jobs—that even a regular old jet jockey would get the nod! Mark hoped so, for his father's sake.

"That could be. Only—"

"Only what, Dad?"

The major chewed his lip briefly. "Only I keep wondering about these streaks right here... along the side of the life boat. That hull is incredibly tough, yet some terrific heat seems to have scorched it."

"Heat... from entering the atmosphere?"

"I don't think so. I have a hunch that it came from some kind of weapons fire."

Mark blinked a few times. "But... that would mean—"

"Hey you two Bamfords!" Alex called from the living room. "Get in here and watch this! They're about to land!"

Dad stood up and gave Mark's shoulder a squeeze as he walked past, ready to leave the photos and just play spectator for a while, as history was made onscreen. But Mark hesitated, lingering to stare down at one picture showing tracks of burnt and melted ceramic—streaks of damage along a gleaming shell.

Columbus is rowing ashore and natives are partying on the beach, he thought, watching festive throngs gather in New York.

Not everybody was unworried. Would the big descent craft arrest its plummet atop a roaring column of rocket flames, belying their assurance of a gentle landing? Standards could differ, after all. Setting a whole city ablaze might be their idea of 'minor damage'.

Or would they intimidate aboriginal Earthlings by hovering overhead, dauntingly silent, as portrayed in countless sci-fi films?

Antigravity is impossible, Na-bistaka had maintained, dismissing the very notion as another useless 'larval fantasy.'

Well, okay then. Mark pondered. Let's see what you have instead.

"We've got visual sighting," said one announcer. Cameras began showing a clear disk whose color changed as it cooled, from bright blue, hard to make out against the sky, down to fiercely bright green and then an iridescent yellow-red. As descent brought it closer, commentators pointed out that the configuration only remotely resembled legendary 'flying saucers' that people claimed to have seen over generations. There were no cupolas or bulges or flashing lights, for instance. Nor did it dart about. Progress was swift but also ponderous, natural.

Above New Jersey, the space vessel dropped below the speed of sound, flying no more than a thousand feet or so overhead. Local citizens under the path reported sudden blasts of hot air, followed by manic cyclones or dust-devils. Leaves and tree-branches whirled in its wake.

"So, it stays up by blasting air downward," Major Bamford deduced with a nod. "Just as we thought. No magical suspensor beams or gravity pulsors. They use Newton's Law as we do— though the *energy source* for such a system…"

Mark saw a gleam of ambition in his father's eye. He wanted a close look at whatever powered that ship.

The Garubis vessel slowed down to a relative crawl over the Hudson, surrounded by federal helicopters that kept swarms of news-choppers at bay. Below, the river's surface bucked and spumed, creating a low, artificial fog.

When that thing touches down in Unity Park, it'll sure make a mess of the Heroes Memorial, Mark thought. On the other hand, statues can be replaced.

Then, still several hundred meters short of Manhattan, the ship halted—hovering on a column of hot, pressurized air. A large panel slid aside, revealing an opening along one flank.

Suddenly, a stream of objects spewed out, hundreds of them, perhaps thousands, all streaking toward New York!

"My God," said Barry. "Are those *missiles?* Could they be attacking?"

"Don't be silly," responded Alex, though her voice quavered. "There must be another explanation."

Mark winced as the horde of cylindrical-shaped objects swooped down toward the cameras in Unity Park, raising shrieks of alarm from the surrounding crowd. For several seconds he didn't breathe...

...until abrupt *order* emerged out of the decelerating objects—each of them now visibly hollow inside. Several dozen of the cylinders plummeted to the park's hard loam, sinking deep. Others followed, clamping onto the tops of those that came before, as they were topped in turn, stacking upon each other, one at a time.

Rapidly, three *spires* began to form—equidistant from each other—rising with uncanny speed.

"It's a self-assembling platform!" Barry announced, crouching to get a better look.

It took less than a minute for the cloud of darting cylinders to visibly shrink, as scores and then hundreds of automatic drones piled higher, aggregating themselves neatly into three steeples that leaned slightly inward, toward each other. The crowd below changed its tone just as rapidly, shifting from fear to awe, and then delight, watching three delicate minarets climb higher and higher, soon topping the nearest of Manhattan's skyscrapers.

Now the great disk of the landing craft started moving in, leaving behind the fog it had kicked up from the Hudson's waters. The spindly platform was ready, a towering tripod almost three hundred meters high, casting long afternoon shadows all the way past Wall Street to the East River. By the time the Lander fully settled in place, shutting down its roaring engines, Mark realized—the Garubis had not lied. They said they would come down in a densely populated Earth-city without causing any damage.

Except to our egos, he thought.

Who needs anti-gravity when you can do stuff like that?

The visitors had made it clear—things were to be done in a specific order.

First, repatriate Na-bistaka. Then talk.

That seemed a little churlish, by human standards. It might have been more reassuring to share greetings and pleasantries along the way. Have a little ceremony. Exchange some gifts. Offer them keys to the city.

("No!" One expert objected. "They might take the 'key' symbolism literally!")

The Jersey subway tunnel had been closed all day, in order to bring the xeno guest-castaway from the airport by a safe route—one terminating in the secure zone just beneath the titanic landing tower. Much of the world's population watched as Na-bistaka, in his enveloping scarlet gown, rode a tram underneath the Hudson with about a dozen escorting dignitaries from the highest levels of human society. Then escalators carried the group upward through a vacant commuter station, all the way to the surface plaza—whereupon his appearance triggered an eruption of noisy cheers from the surrounding throng, and the thousands more peering from buildings on all sides.

There on the expansive tiled piazza, the Heroes Memorial seemed dwarfed underneath the towering Garubis tripod. Spindly legs flexed as individual machines that made up the structure adjusted automatically to the tug and push of the wind. (Technical experts calculated, breathlessly, that each of the three hollow pillars might weigh less than a city bus!)

The overall effect was to make the quivering tripod look alive, as if ready to advance on legs nearly a thousand feet tall.

"The Martians in H.G. Wells used tall tripods, too—" commented Barry, and he seemed about to add more, till Alex hushed him.

Na-bistaka and Earth's accompanying emissaries now approached one of these towering limbs. The crowd hushed as an opening appeared, a *door* in the bottommost cylinder at the plaza level, revealing a dimly-lit elevator car.

Nobody emerged. No one could be glimpsed inside.

Quickening his stride with apparent eagerness, Na-bistaka moved ahead of his human escorts, who followed nervously. Without pausing, the scarlet-clad alien then entered the waiting lift without a word.

He did not even turn around as the doors closed behind him, leaving the Mayor of New York, the Vice-President of the United States, the Secretary General of the United Nations, and Imam Suleiman—representative of the Ecumenical Council of Faiths— all just standing there.

For several stunned minutes, none of them moved. Nobody seemed willing to be first.

Eventually, as twilight began to fall, the disappointed dignitaries began drifting away—robbed of their former dignity.

"Well," summed up Alexandra Behr, tossing a piece of popcorn in her mouth. "*That* was rude."

As the initial shock wore off, some TV commentators tried

to make excuses for the Garubis, repeating the aphorism—*Do not judge others by your own values. Their ways may be different. We must allow for aliens having unique and possibly strange notions of courtesy.*

That refrain continued for a while, on every broadcast and cable channel... until one person finally dared to speak up with a dissenting point of view.

It was the woman college professor Mark had seen earlier, who had urged that humanity stay both bold and well-grounded.

"Hogwash!" she muttered now.

"Clearly and logically, it's up to any visitor to learn and adjust to native customs, and *we're* the natives, here! They're supposed to be the smart, sophisticated ones, right? Experienced at contact? Yet *we* took care of all the language translation difficulties. We took pains to learn the Xeno's needs. We transmitted the Message, rolled out the red carpet and offered every hospitality...."

She had to stop, half-choked with anger, taking a moment before resuming.

"They're guests in our home, and one *should* accommodate guests—even bend over backwards. But we've done all that, and more!

"Let's not bend over so far now that we can't see the obvious.

"Friends and fellow Earthlings... I'm afraid our *guests* have just peed on our carpet."

No one was especially surprised, then, to hear the engines of the landing craft start to warm up. National guardsmen pushed and the crowd backed away as hot wind blasted down from the tripod, sending billows of dust whipping down the handmade canyons of Manhattan.

"We should have insisted on a trade," Barry Tang said. "Demanded rent. A rescue fee! Kept ahold of the little jerk till they paid some of that old *quid pro quo*."

"I guess so," Mark sighed. It was obvious now, in retrospect.

And yet, generosity had felt so *right*. To offer hospitality and kindness without any overt sign of greed. For the last month or so, the whole world had seemed astonished and rather pleased with its own new, altruistic attitude. Defying all the cynics who routinely despised human nature, most people took the high road out of a sense of...

Well, maybe it was pride.

We may be poor natives. But we do have honor. Honor that we either ignored or horribly abused among ourselves, for all of recorded time. Still, it existed. All cultures shared the core notions.

Underneath everything, when we decide to pay attention, that honor may be stronger than we ever suspected.

Only now, was that turning out to be a mistake, after all?

The disk lifted from its perch atop the towering tripod, and at once the three-legged platform started dissolving, from the top down, into countless small-hollow drones that swirled to join a spinning cloud. Like a genie re-entering its lamp, the swarm drew inward, converging and funnelling to the belly of the hovering craft. When every last one had been recovered, the vessel turned southeast to cruise past the Statue of Liberty, climbing as it accelerated over the Atlantic.

People in Manhattan—and on all continents—watched in sour disappointment. There would be no speeches today. No welcoming ceremonies. No negotiations.

No party.

Then came a final surprise.

Even as the lander passed out of sight, a chuttering sound abruptly surged from every radio and television set, broadcast by the giant Garubis star galleon, high overhead. Caught by surprise, most networks needed a few moments to seek help with translation. A group of amateur linguists from Manilla beat all the universities and government agencies by several seconds, providing a first English-language version of the aliens' announcement.

We acknowledge that you have done us a service.
We acknowledge that we are in your debt.

The pause that followed might have been deliberate. Or simply punctuation. For emphasis.

We hate being indebted to vermin.

Mark's jaw dropped. Nor was he alone. There had to be something wrong with the translation! Perhaps it was somebody's idea of a joke.

Only then alternate versions began appearing on different channels—from the U.S. government and from academics who had worked directly with Na-bistaka. All paraphrasings of the Garubis broadcast converged on the same general meaning.

We shall discharge this debt as soon as possible.

We shall repay you with something of high value
from the List of Traditional Restitutions
For The Young And Hungry.

We shall do this before your planet spins another six times.
Then, in gladness, we will depart.
And then try to expunge
memory of your noxious odors.

For the longest time, not a single pundit or commentator spoke. The airwaves of Planet Earth were more quiet than they had been in generations. Perhaps since the days of Marconi.

Oh, this wasn't the very worst possible kind of alien contact.

But almost without any doubt it was the most insulting.

Of course, not everybody saw things the same way. Barry

Tang finally broke the silence in the Bamford home with a chortle of eagerness.

"Cool!" he said, rubbing his hands avariciously.

"I wonder what they're gonna give us."

Study Hall   7

Much to Mark's surprise, life went on during the week that followed.

At Twenty-Nine Palms High School, preparations went into high gear for both Prom night and the Spring Desert Festival. Nearly all of the posters depicting merry gray aliens were defaced by vandals, so Principal Jeffers ordered a change in theme. Some leftover decorations from last year's "Underwater Charm" dance were hastily gussied up—by the small minority of students who cared about such things.

As the big day approached, carnival people arrived in a small caravan of trucks to begin setting up a striped tent and a compact amusement park at one end of the athletic field, complete with coin-pitch booths (for fundraising) and a couple of high-intensity Hurl Rides. There was even an animal act, with some trained dogs and a performing chimp. The same carnies—tattooed and surly, but generally harmless—had been doing the desert festival at TNPHS for years.

With midterms over, seniors started gathering in clusters on the school steps, signing yearbooks and vowing to keep in touch after dispersing to various colleges, or else employed independence. Meanwhile, Mark's fellow juniors felt the approach of their own turn at the top of the school totem pole. Some began firing up campaigns for office in the coming school elections.

Still, any resemblance to normality was superficial. Teens

who never used to pay attention to current events—even those who couldn't name a senator or governor—now checked their pocket web-readers between classes, in case some news had come down from the orbiting starship.

Everyone knew that Friday would be the big day. One that might change the world. It roused a lot of contradictory feelings.

While bagging groceries at Food King, Mark felt keenly aware of how many people eyed him—not just kids from TNPHS, but townspeople in general. Some offered sour looks, as if the rudeness shown by Na-bistaka's folk had somehow been his fault. Others scanned the tabloid magazines that lined his checkout counter. Every issue blared speculations about what *The Gift* would turn out to be. Conjectures ranged from cancer cures to smart pills, from the secret of life to a new weight-loss diet that really works. Sometimes, people reading these headlines would smile at Mark, or pat him on the back as they departed. Others left oversized tips at his bagging station.

The first time that happened, Mark put every nickel into the collection bin for Muscular Dystrophy. After that, he gave all the accumulated tips to a homeless lady he often saw on the corner, roaming with her possessions piled in a shopping cart. Her reaction, to mutter and look away, suited him fine.

One thing Mark knew for certain—if the aliens' *Gift* turned out to be a disappointment, he was going to have to leave the town of Twenty Nine Palms. Maybe California. Hell, was there any place on Earth where he could hide, if humanity didn't like the Garubis' notion of 'repayment'?

A gift appropriate for vermin. Yeah, that boded well. Right. Maybe it was already time to start packing.

"What would *you* ask for?" Mr. Clements demanded, during history class, right after that fizzled 'first contact' was broadcast live from New York on a fateful Saturday night. The assignment: think up your own best guess about the Gift and come prepared to defend your choice on Wednesday—just two days before the world would find out the truth.

It was kind of hard to concentrate at the climbing wall.

True, the girls soccer team had vanished—with their playing field given over to the Winter Carnival—and no jocks were using weights below. It seemed a good time for the X Team to get some practice in.

Only this time there was so much noise and bustle nearby, as big roustabouts shouted, hammering pegs into the ground, setting up tents and amusement rides. In recent years, the little fair had grown much bigger than a High School homecoming dance, drawing in pretty much the whole valley on the second night. And now the carnies were adding even more, hoping the brief notoriety of TwentyNine Palms might draw in tourists from the coast.

I hope not, Mark thought, perhaps a bit disloyally. It was the school's biggest fundraiser and this year, the climbing wall would be a part of it, raising money for X Team shirts and sweats. Even so, he didn't hanker to see the outside world return, with its glaring scrutiny.

"Come on, Bamford! You're on the clock!"

This time it was Froggi Hayashi egging him on, from just overhead. *All right.* Mark concentrated. *Stick to the rhythm.*

Left foot goes to the Doorknob... set it... now shift weight and PUSH as left hand shoots for the Wedgie... jam it good...

He had given nicknames to every hand and foothold in the memorized route. Not very realistic, of course. In life, the authentic challenge always comes from variety and *surprise*, with no ascent ever the same twice. But this route was part of the standardized prelims. A pure speed race. Moving systematically and by rote, he quickly made it to the top with only a minimum of sweat.

Alex released Mark's harness and Barry Tang, who had attached himself to the team as equipment manager, quickly coiled the rope. "Not bad," Froggi said, looking at his stopwatch. He showed the time to the Hammar twins, Nick and Greg.

"I guess you won't shame us," Greg Hammar commented.

Mark glanced at the time. *Shame us? Only Alex is quicker. And she's half spider. We'll do fine at the first match… if that sort of thing matters anymore.*

Churning at the back of his mind was the same thing distracting nearly everybody else—how the Garubis "gift" might change everything.

Already there were voices, in the media and among leading thinkers, who seriously proposed that humanity should *refuse* the gratuity. And not just out of pride or xenophobia. After all, how could people trust a benefaction given by aliens who call your kind "vermin"? No matter how attractive the dingus turned out to be, you had to worry and wonder. Could it wind up being like the bait in a mousetrap? Or the honeyed ingredient in roach poison? Even some of those who had been most enthusiastic were now suggesting that the Gift be extensively tested… perhaps on an isolated island, or even the Moon… before exposing humanity and Earth as a whole.

Alex said that her parents were still in a state of shock. After all of their hard work, taking care of Na-Bistaka, clearly they had allowed their hopes to climb, like kids before a birthday. Expectations of something like gratitude. Or at least a pat on the head.

If the others were pensive, Froggi Hayashi seemed unflappable, true to the spirit of X. "Come on," he said, after they were finished cleaning up and the Hammar boys hurried off to meet their ride.

"Bring your gear. I got a surprise for you guys."

Our gear? Mark shouldered a rope and his bag of climbing tools, glancing at Alex, who shrugged, as much in the dark as he was. Her tank top exposed shoulders that were a tad more ripped—more muscular—than Mark generally found attractive in a girl. Still, on Alex it seemed right somehow.

Perhaps sensing scrutiny, she threw on a sweatshirt and stepped after Froggi, letting Mark and Barry take up the rear. Soon they were approaching the main building of Twenty-Nine Palms High, apparently empty as a ghost town, an hour after the student throng made its daily escape.

"I've checked carefully," the X Boy said, stopping next to the Bell Tower—a decorative feature that jutted from one end of the two story structure, giving it a faux, California Mission feel. There had never been a bell.

"This is a total blind spot. Nobody can see us here, except from the direction we just came."

Mark looked around. It seemed plausible. "So?"

Froggi dumped his gear and started chalking his hands.

"So? I'm going up. Anyone else coming?"

Mark stared at the boy, and then at the planned route. There were very few holds or protrusions. "Has anybody done it before?"

"Doubt it. The tower's only a couple of years old and I figure we would of heard. I'm gonna carve my initials where nobody but another climber can see." Froggi whipped out a carving chisel that was almost certainly against campus zero-tolerance rules. "Relax, I didn't smuggle a weapon on campus. I borrowed this from wood shop."

Mark wasn't sure the principal would accept that distinction. But Alex stepped up.

"I'm in," she said.

Really? Mark blinked at her. Then Barry Tang eagerly spoke. "I'll go topside and belay," he said, tucking a rope inside his bulky jacket.

"Don't get caught!" Froggi called after, as Barry hurried off, disappearing around a corner. The X boy secured his chalk bag and straightened his knit cap before stepping inside a narrow space—barely a decorative niche—between the jutting tower and the building proper.

"Chimney ascent," Mark commented, feeling a rising sense of appreciation... against his better judgement. "It's been a long time."

Alex nodded. "It does seem kinda dumb to call ourselves a *climbing team* when all we've done is a wimpy, artificial knob-wall. I was gonna take you all out to some nice pipes and crevices in Joshua Tree, over break. But this is cool, too."

Well, well, Mark thought, pondering her tone. *Look at Miss Nonconformist.* Alex was normally kind of proper. But maybe she felt this was her moment to prove something. "Wing stretching" as Dad called it. Teen rebellion didn't always make sense. Sometimes, it wan't even clear what you were trying to prove.

Okay, he thought, peering up at the route that Froggi proposed. *What's the worst that can happen?*

Mark instantly regretted posing it that way. He rephrased the question in his mind. *How much trouble can we get into?*

Like all climbers, from amateur to pro, he knew about legendary "urban ascents," when dashing daredevils challenged skyscrapers like the Chicago Sears Tower, transfixing newscams and millions of viewers around the world. Security experts kept erecting barriers to prevent such stunts, and even those who succeeded were sure to be arrested, upon reaching the top. Still, there seemed to be an unwritten set of conventions about what kind of punishment you could expect. If no one else was endangered, if no property got harmed, and assuming no greedy or nasty motives were involved, it often came down to a couple of nights in jail, a modest fine, and some weeks assigned to community service. In one famous case, that meant visiting school assemblies, preaching the value of enthusiasm and skill and being good at *something*.

Mark wondered. *Does this qualify? Or could we all get suspended?* Nowadays, there was often a blurry boundary between avid self-expression and something that deserved *zero-tolerance*.

"Watch out below!" A hoarse whisper floated down from the bell tower, just ahead of a coiled end of rope. While Froggi clamped in with his harness, Mark hoped that Barry remembered how to tie off and belay without an auto-tensioner. *Maybe I should have gone up to handle it.*

Maybe I should now.

But Hayashi was already inside the niche, wedging his back against one side while bracing his climbing shoes against the other, shifting one foot and then the other as he wormed his way upward along both gritty surfaces.

Mark looked closely at the wall, ready to call a halt if the surface looked damaged—one sure way to turn a "harmless stunt" into hooligan vandalism. But it seemed to be good crete, not crumbly stucco. There were no scars, even when Froggi scuffed hard.

Backing out to look around, Mark checked for anyone passing by. Mr. Perez, the campus patrolman, would be on duty until six. But the retired cop was so preoccupied, watching every move the carnies made, that he ought to be busy for a while.

Froggi moved pretty quickly. Not too surprising, given his strength and small, wiry frame. He was arching and wriggling and then arching again, driving himself upward in a repetitious rhythm that would never work in a real rock chimney, with countless jagged variations and tricky surfaces that require careful evaluation and planning. *Typical X-stuff,* Mark figured. For all of their bravado, these urban sportsmen relied on the predictable smoothness of their skateboard half-pipes and metro steets. None of nature's wild unpredictability.

"Move it, Bam," Alex said, pushing past Mark and tossing her sweatshirt at him. "Use your slot or lose it."

Dang, girl, he thought. *What'd I do to you?*

Violating proper procedure, Alex started bracing herself in before Froggi even made it to the top. Of course, the chances of Hayashi falling onto her were small, given a decent belay. Still.

"Almost... there..." Froggi announced, and fumbled for the chisel in his pocket. Mark watched the process warily, positioning himself in case the boy dropped his tool. If it plummeted toward

Alex, Mark would have just a split second to knock it aside. *This is stupid. You don't rush things. Not even in a dopey little stunt.*

Alex seemed oblivious to any danger... or to a sprinkle of wood shavings that floated down, as Froggi carved a quick pair of initials into his chosen spot under the cornice ledge, visible only to those who would follow their path, in coming years. Hardly a case of immoral "vandalism". But if that chisel fell toward Alex—

Mark braced himself, anxiously, ready to swat it out of space...

...till Hayashi grunted with satisfaction, twirled the tool, and jabbed it hard into the wooden eave, leaving it for the next person. Pretty deep. Mark relaxed a little.

"Gritty," Alex commented as she set her back and feet in place, testing her strength against both walls of the chimney. Without sleeves, the girl abraded her shoulders every time she arched her back to shimmy higher.

"You should wear this." He offered the sweatshirt and she seemed to ponder for a moment... till a hoarse laugh from above announced Froggi's final arrival, scrambling over the rim with Barry's help, into the bell tower cupola. The rope soon tumbled down in a loop that uncoiled all the way to Alex. Forgetting any discomfort, she eagerly connected it to her harness, then took three deep breaths, as Mark checked it. The moment he nodded, she started up—taking one short footstep, another, then heaving her pelvis upward and wriggling to bring her shoulders and back along... all without ever losing contact with either side of the narrow slot.

For some pleople, it might seem an awkward process. But Alex made it look natural. In fact, she appeared more graceful right now than she did while just walking around... a wry observation that made Mark smile... and that he decided to keep to himself.

We are, each of us, many people inside.

The thought seemed to rise within his mind, as if out of no-where. Watching Alex push her way up the chimney, Mark felt like at least a dozen different individuals.

A protective older friend, or brother, wary in case she slipped—

A comrade who was charged with guarding this little band against discovery, by keeping a lookout for anyone passing too close—

A student with a B average, who did not need a black mark on his record, wishing he had found the nerve to say no—

And a rebel who was sick of always being Mr. Responsible... as if that trait ever paid off in any big way—

Plus yet another guy, stirring inside, who—almost in spite of himself—found that Alex's athletic ascent, writhing and grunting and far from feminine, nevertheless had an alluring and strangely attractive quality. A fascination to the eye, as well as to some of the hormonal drives that had been surging through his body, of late...

He pushed those thoughts aside, calling upon an image of Helene Shockley. There. Now that was an obsession. It felt more naturally erotic and *far* less confusing.

"Half of the decisions you'll make in life, son—" his father once said to Mark *"—the good choices and the bad ones, will often boil down to one thing. Picking which of your inner selves shall get to be in change, at any given time."*

Mark shook his head, sharply. The whole world had been lecturing him, for months now. The last thing he needed was to get it from his own damn mind.

There was one antidote to uncomfortable thoughts. *Action.* Motion and the satisfaction of actually getting something done! So, before Alex was more than halfway up, he decided on impulse. Stepping into the niche between the bell tower and the main wall, Mark settled his back against one wall, feeling sharp grit poke through the fabric of the flannel shirt.

Well, if Alex could take it, he sure could.

Here goes.

First one foot met the opposite wall and pressed hard... then the other. It was a tighter fit for Mark than it had been for the other two, requiring more lateral force and muscle tension, but also offering him greater range of movement than Froggi or Alex had. *This shouldn't be too hard.* Settling in, he took a short step, wriggled his back upward, moved the other foot, and looked up.

Alex was quite a bit higher, only about two meters short of the top. Her arms and legs glistened with sweat and there were abrasion marks—scratches—from her shoulders to her elbows. She had slowed a bit, but seemed to have things under control.

Of course, strictly speaking, he shouldn't be here in the slot. Not with another climber above and no rope of his own. But it would only be the first few minutes and this really did feel pretty easy.

It *was* easy, at first. Step. Step. Arch and press with the arms. Wriggle higher. Then repeat. Step. Step. Arch and press with the arms. Wriggle higher. Then repeat. As he had expected, it was pretty mindless, without any of the tricky variety of a natural chimney. In fact, Mark soon found he was catching up with Alex. One of the less mature corners of his mind took some satisfaction. This'll show her.

Soon, the sophomore girl was in reach of Froggi's chisel. Setting herself solidly in place, she reached for it—

—when suddenly a sound floated upward from below and not too far away. Mark halted his writhing ascent to listen.

Footsteps on the nearby path. Someone whistling a nondescript tune.

From overheard, Mark heard Barry Tang's unmistakable, worried whisper. "Sh! Everybody quiet!"

What do I do? Mark pondered. *Drop back down, step out and try to distract whoever it is?*

Remain where I am, keeping as still as possible?

The footsteps drew nearer. The whistle, louder. Mark decided.

Hurry on up. That way, I'll be well above eye-level, even if someone glances inside the niche.

Somewhere inside, a little voice complained. This was probably the wrong choice. Still, *Alex* seemed to agree. Even as Mark

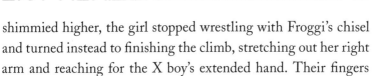

shimmied higher, the girl stopped wrestling with Froggi's chisel and turned instead to finishing the climb, stretching out her right arm and reaching for the X boy's extended hand. Their fingers brushed, grabbed for each other, found a grip. Froggi started to pull her up…

"Give her slack!" He whispered over his shoulder at Barry.

No, don't! But Mark's voice would not come. Caught in an awkward position, his chest had no room to push the words out.

Froggi's grip on her arm did not look—

It all happened in a blur. Alex surrendered her chimney bridge, letting herself swing outward and dangle, giving Froggi's hold more trust than it deserved. Hayashi groaned at the sudden weight. Alex reached with her other arm and scrambled for the lip of the balcony, where Barry was trying to help clutch at her…

…letting go of his rope belay.…

…just an instant before Alex lost her grip and fell.

Letting out a cry as he twisted aside, Mark shot out his right hand out to grab at her, mid-plummet. He felt a crashing impact and, for an instant, Alex was actually *in his arm,* caught and held, swinging wildly as her eyes briefly met his. Mark's shoulder burned from pressure against the gritty wall, desperately holding them both up.

But it was only for a second or two. Then his hold broke. She fell away, resuming her rush to the ground. Mark let out a sob and braced himself to hear a crunching noise.

But the sound of impact came much softer than expected. Was it adrenaline or the pounding in his chest, that muffled the blow when she struck ground? Mark wriggled back into some kind of stable position and then—through speckled vision—forced himself to look down.

There was Alex. Safe, it seemed. In the arms of a burly man with wiry, tattooed shoulders and a dark, scraggly beard. At a glance, you could tell he was either one of the carnies or some kind of biker—probably both, holding Alex as if she weighed almost nothing.

up-CHUCK said a patch on the big fellow's denim shirt.

After a moment or two, while the girl caught her breath, he released Alex, depositing her on her own two feet, then scanned Mark and the other two boys, gaping down from the tower.

The carny slowly smiled. At first it seemed a friendly expression... that turned wry and disdaining... followed by a dismissive snort. Before anyone could breathe a word of thanks, the man turned and was gone.

It took some minutes for Mark to worm his way back down the narrow chimney-niche between the tower and the main building. By that time, Froggi and Barry had rejoined Alex and were dabbing at her scratched shoulders with some alchohol pads. Nobody said a word. Mark wasn't even aware that he had injuries of his own, till Alex tugged at his shirt to wipe away streaks of blood. The garment wasn't going to be good for much more than the rag box, now.

Everybody was a bit subdued, avoiding eye-contact as they returned their climbing gear to the lock box. Froggi managed to quash any sense of elation over his own accomplishment, though at school tomorrow he would doubtless lead all the other X kids to see the chisel, poking into view under the eave of the bell tower. His signal of priority and a challenge to those who might follow.

Big deal, Mark pondered, sharing a final glance and nod with Alex. Perhaps neither of them would even mention what had happened here. Or what it meant. But on his way home, could still remember the mixed feelings and confusion. The feeling of being many people, *all* of them terribly perplexed.

Maybe the Gift will be something to simplify it all. To cut through the puzzle of life and let people quickly see what's true.

It sounded pretty cool... and yet...

And yet, casting his mind back to the intensity of those moments—and the look on Alex's face when she silent said thanks—Mark wasn't sure that he really regreted all the confusion of growing up. Or anything at all.

Essay
Questions   **8**

The Garubis were punctual. Friday morning, as Mark and his father had breakfast together, all of the world's three thousand channels carried news, bulleted in two hundred languages.

The starship had changed orbits. It now kept station above North America.

"I'd better report to base," Dad said, standing up and taking his plate to the sink. Unspoken was the fact that his experimental team had the most advanced aircraft in the world, incorporating what few bits of alien technology the experts had managed to decipher in three frantic months. If something went wrong today... well, that didn't bear much thinking.

"Stay cool, Dad," Mark said, quashing a tight feeling inside.

"You too, son." His father gave Mark's shoulder a squeeze, harder than usual, then departed. Mark loaded the dishwasher, hoisted his backpack and locked the front door before hopping on his bike.

Students were converging for the last day of school before Winter Festival, but there was none of the usual chatter about who was taking whom to the dance. By the bike racks, and then on the steps leading inside, few people spoke. Dozens of small radios reported that a disk had once again spun off the giant cylinder in space. Another lander was leaving a trail of hot, ionized flame as it circled Earth once on its way down.

In New York, fresh preparations were underway. Perhaps

this time the visitors would choose to talk a bit, when they delivered Earth's "compensation." Nobody—not even the most optimistic—expected much of a party.

Settling into his first class of the day, Mark knew that Mr. Clements had scored a bulls-eye. The topic he assigned on Monday was atop everybody's mind.

The Gift.

"What would *I* ask for?" Dave McCarty groused bitterly. "Why bother thinking about it? They don't plan to ask us what *we* want, obviously. They'll pick something *they* think we need, like grandma sending me hippie clothes every birthday."

Paulina Isfhani raised her hand.

"I'm hoping they'll offer us a way to grow meat without killing animals! We could feed the world with a lot less waste and pain." It was an old topic, but she met the groans of her classmates with defiance. "I'm not surprised they weren't polite to us. We're murderers!"

Mr. Clements quashed further moans, raising both hands. "That's a legitimate hypothesis, Paulina. Any other ideas?"

Jennifer Ledgerwood spoke up, glaring at her ex-boyfriend across the aisle. "How about giving everybody a really good lie detector!"

"Hm, yes," the teacher mused. "That would certainly change politics and commerce... as well as dating. We could discuss that one for a year. Anyone else?"

A rapid series of suggestions burst forth as each student, in turn, seemed to have a special wish.

"Flying cars!"

"Cures for disease and getting old."

"A way to learn stuff without going to school!"

"Something about God?"

"Clean energy."

"I'm hoping for some new cuisine!" announced Marcel Landais. "I am so sick of pizza and burgers and tacos and chow mein. Something really alien and yummy would be nice."

After the laughter died down, Lance Ford had a different suggestion.

"How about a way to, you know, freeze people and thaw them later safely? So they could be fixed when a cure is found for their sickness? Or even if you're *not* sick. You could use it to visit other planets. Or the future, where things'll be better. I bet the Garubis have that, or they couldn't go to the stars."

Some classmates nodded at this logic, but Mark knew the last part was wrong. These aliens didn't need suspended animation. They had faster-than-light transport—*much* faster—in order to have come for Na-bistaka just ten days after being called.

"Do you think people would do that?" Mr. Clements asked, clearly intrigued. "Would healthy folks have themselves frozen in order to sleep out the next century, hoping things will get better? Yes, Arlene?"

The immigrant girl lowered her hand.

"That could be the *only* way to make things better."

"What do you mean?"

"I mean that right now the world's population is so high… it takes all of our resources just to feed people and stay even. I heard one expert predict that we'll have a 'population correction' soon. He seemed so *calm*, talking about how that would bring things back into balance, though a 'correction' like that means two or three billion people dying!"

Arlene turned to look back at the rest of the class.

"Believe me, those billions won't go willingly or peacefully! They will take the rest of us down with them."

Students stared. Nobody had never seen Arlene get so intense.

"Whereas, if we had hibernation—" Mr. Clements prompted, urging her to complete the thought.

"Well… if such a technique proved safe and easy and cheap enough… those same billions of people might *choose* to get out of the way, calmly sleeping and waiting it out. Meanwhile, others could use the new sup… srup…"

"Surplus?"

"Yes, *surplus.* Those who stay awake would have to promise to use the surplus this created, to solve problems! Invest in new cities and technologies. Clean up the environment. Make a paradise for the sleepers to wake into!"

Mark couldn't help blinking in wonder. Arlene's growing confidence had burst through some inner threshold. From a shy immigrant kid speaking broken English, she was turning into a strong person with formidable views... if somewhat unnerving ones.

Mr. Clements mused. "I think I once read a story about that very scenario."

More groans. Ever since the world turned upside down that fateful Thursday, he kept recalling 'classic' science fiction tales about First Contact. Their variety appeared limitless, in film or book or magazine, and Mr. Clements seemed to know them all.

"I think it was written by Offutt and Lyon. Those two also wrote a scenario even more relevant to our present situation. Let me see if I can remember—I think it was about aliens who come to Earth in need of something. I don't know—maybe some chemical from daisies—it doesn't really matter.

"In this story, they offer to *buy* the thing they want, but Earth's appointed negotiator acts coy. So they up their offer, from a new power source all the way to a couple of used starships! World leaders want to leap at this, but the negotiator figures the visitors are eager, maybe even desperate. They really need this thing we have. He also figures that they are still offering the equivalent of glass beads.

"So he finally decides what to demand from them."

The teacher paused and Mark found himself waiting, tensely.

"Yeah?" Hodge Takahashi finally urged, voice edgy with impatience.

Mr. Clements smiled.

"Finally, the negotiator insists on one price for the item the aliens need. He demands that the visitors say, *please.*"

Hodge blinked a couple of times, as confused as his classmates.

"That's... dumb."

"Is it?" Mr. Clements shrugged. "In the story, that one demand sends the aliens into a tizzy. They offer a dozen *new* starships. 'Anything but that,' they cry. 'Don't make us say please.'"

"That doesn't make sense!"

"Oh, but it does," Helene Shockley's voice murmured behind Mark. He turned to see her hand raised, jingling copper bracelets. "I think I see what the author was getting at."

Mark saw it, too. But he had vowed to stay out of these *sci fi* discussions. Talk about aliens only churned his stomach. He wished the class would go back to ancient European History.

"You only say *please* when you talk to equals," Helene explained. "Or those close to being equal If someone asks you 'please' for something they need, it means you get to do the same."

Then her voice dropped a little. "At least... that's what I think the author might have meant."

Mr. Clements nodded. "That seems reasonable. Can anyone see parallels between this story and what's happening today? Mr. Bamford?"

Mark sighed. "The Garubis think we're trash. That's all."

"But that's *not* all, Mark," Helene protested. "If we had *acted* like trash, they'd have felt just fine about snubbing us, or maybe doing something worse. But we surprised them."

"Maybe because our movies always show people behaving so badly," Trevor suggested. "All the TV and stuff that they watched from space... it made them expect that we'd act a lot more stupid. A lot worse."

Helene nodded. "Maybe. Anyway, now, according to some kind of Galactic code—maybe a law or tradition—they have to treat us better than they really want to. That *means* something."

"Yeah," Mark muttered, with unexpected vehemence. "It means now they hate us. They'll hand over some booby prize and then think hard about ways to get even with us for embarrassing them. That's what lots of humans would do, admit it!"

She met his gaze. "Well... then we just have to hope they aren't like *lots* of humans."

Again, Mark wondered if Helene was putting some kind of meaning into her words—something personal. It might be solved if he had the courage to talk to her. On the other hand, she seemed happy with her Student Body President boyfriend—they were Prom Couple—so what was there to talk about?

Maybe next year, when Scott Tepper is in college....

Before he could reply, a low murmur intruded, growing louder outside the classroom. A mutter of human voices. It grew louder. Dave McCarty flipped open his web-unit. He, too, started babbling.

"The lander! They say it's *not* aimed for New York."

Normally, it was an infraction to open a media device in class. But not today. Mr. Clements stepped forward. "Where do they say—"

"When it passed Hawaii the trajectory seemed bound for Southern California. Mojave Desert."

Which makes it easy to guess what the precise target is, Mark realized. *The Contact Center. Those white domes at the end of a runway, where Na-bistaka accepted our hospitality and every comfort we could provide.*

Dad will get a front row seat. Maybe he'll be first to see this "Gift" when they roll it out. Unless he's scrambled and airborne when it comes.

By this time the TV in the corner of the room was on, showing one network's quick estimate of the glide path. Sure enough, it terminated just north of Joshua Tree National Monument—in the vicinity of Twenty-Nine Palms, California.

Doubtless, every helicopter in Los Angeles would be on its way here in moments, carrying frantic journalists back to their old stake-out.

When the period bell rang, some students wandered out and a few others drifted in, as if expecting the next class to begin as usual. It didn't, of course. Any semblance of a normal schedule was completely forgotten as teachers and students alike clustered around the nearest media source. That is, until a deep-throated *thunder* rattled the windows and rocked the sky, much lower and more ominous than the familiar sonic booms of USAF jets.

Suddenly, every artificial medium was abandoned. Students, teachers and staff poured outdoors, shading their eyes against the glare as sharp sunlight reflected off a disklike object, now creeping slowly from the west amid a rising growl.

Despite his cynicism, Mark found it astonishing to see a Garubis vessel up close. It made a vision far lovelier than he had expected from televised images. In fact, for a minute or two he actually felt... well... privileged. The sheer beauty of the glistening craft—still emitting a glow from its fiery path through the atmosphere—went beyond any issue he might have with the people flying it.

Alex felt the same way.

"Something to tell the grandchildren, eh?" she said, nudging Mark as she joined him on the front steps.

"Uh huh." And yet, squinting, Mark found himself starting to worry. Something seemed wrong about the ship's slow trajectory across the sky. Something unexpected.

They were joined by Barry Tang who asked Alex. "Isn't your mother at the Contact Center?"

"Yeah. She was disappointed not to be part of the Eastern Team, but now she'll be right there when history is made! Mark's father, too. We'll get first-hand stories."

"Maybe," Mark commented amid a growing concern, as he watched the lander's puzzling approach pattern. Barry saved him from having to say it aloud.

"Is it just me?" the younger boy mused. "Or does it look like that ship is—"

Slowing down a bit too much, Mark thought as Barry fell silent. *And it's not on a direct course for the air base.*

In fact, the huge flying craft did not waver a bit, left or right, as it came straight at them. From this shortened distance, that meant the lander couldn't be heading for the Contact Center, five miles to the north.

It's... coming here.

Seconds later that fact grew obvious to everyone, as a door opened in the side of the great disk, vomiting a cloud of cylindrical drones that came swooping toward the town. This time, everyone knew about the Garubis style of landing. But it was one thing to watch on TV and quite another for the flurry of hollow tubes to hurtle toward *you,* like a swarm of huge, angry bees.

People screamed. Quite a few started to run, but the whirling cyclone of flying things now surrounded several city blocks. It took more courage to approach the perimeter than to retreat inside the school.

Even from a height of a thousand feet, exhaust blasting down from the hovering lander felt uncomfortably hot. Only a hardy minority of students and staff remained outside to watch three spindly-but-massive legs rapidly take shape, self-assembling and climbing swiftly into the sky. One pillar slanted upward from the Food King's parking lot. A second crushed a hapless semi-trailer to bits, next to the Shell station. The third spire set carnival dogs yelping madly as it grew upward from the athletic field.

"I guess—" Barry stammered. "I g-guess they're gonna give the... the Gift to—"

"—to *us.*" Alex finished the thought for him. "Damn. It better be something cool."

Speaking of cool, Mark admired how Alex was keeping hers. Then he caught her glancing up at him and realized. *She thinks the same thing about me.*

Barely more than a minute after it began, the tripod was finished self-assembling and the lander had begun settling quickly

into place, at least two hundred meters overhead. The blast of warm air tapered off and then ceased...

...but not a low hum that Mark had noticed for some time now. It seemed to vibrate his very innards.

Now that the razor cloud of intimidating drones was gone, some people moved. A few ran for the perimeter—Mark noticed Tom Spencer, not hanging around to see what his reward might be for rescuing a stranded creature from the desert sands. Others hurried *forward,* skooting in from the town, driven more by excitement than fear.

Go or stay? he asked himself, as the vibration seemed to intensify, plucking his bones like strings. Mark knew, somehow, that Alex and Barry would follow, whatever he chose to do.

Decide now.

Parental Notification 9

Rushing from the white dome of the Contact Center, Dr. Karen Behr flashed her credentials and commandeered a place aboard one of the helicopters rising from the nearby airstrip. Voices yammered frantic questions in her ear via a secure link to other members of her team, assembled in New York.

"I don't know anything yet!" she shouted as the chopper pilot set blades spinning. "The tripod stands just south of here, right over the town! No, we haven't heard a peep from the lander. Has there been anything from the Mother Ship?"

"Nothing at all."

Lifting off, the copter soon gave her a better perspective. The alien tower-platform had seemed impressive last Saturday, standing beside Manhattan's skyscrapers. Now, above the open desert, it resembled a mountain, a stool for gods, a giant *fork* stuck in the Earth. Air force planes and news copters buzzing nearby only struck home the scale of the thing. They were gnats. Less than gnats.

"Oh dear lord," she murmured as they gained enough altitude to look down—at an angle—upon the little city of Twenty Nine Palms. "It's standing right over my daughter's school."

The helicopter pitched and bucked.

"Keep it still!" One of Karen's associates demanded, trying to aim instruments at the spacecraft.

"Something's screwing the electronics," the pilot snapped. Karen noticed several cockpit meters twitching to the same rhythm of static she heard in her headset, a rhythm that seemed also to penetrate her skin.

Despite the noise, New York kept hurling frantic questions.

"I don't know!" She repeated. "But I think something's about to happen!"

More frenzied queries rattled her ears, but she could only answer with a low cry as the Garubis lander shuddered, causing the tripod to tremble visibly. It changed *color* before her eyes, sliding along the spectrum from reddish toward yellow, green and finally intense blue.

Then, from the vessel's rim, there fell a curtain of dazzling light, dripping slowly as if liquid. In terrified dismay, Karen saw the radiant cone broaden—catching two of the circling aircraft in its hem, sending them a-tumble toward the nearby desert —then contract to fit snugly within the space encompassed by the tripod legs. It was hard to look at the fierce illumination, which seemed to solidify somehow, into a bubble of palpable brilliance.

A *jolt* shook the chopper. The pilot struggled, throwing his throttle to full and climbing even as a shock wave—visible as *ripple* in the air—caught up and plowed into them. For several moments, Karen held on for dear life as they dipped, rattled and shook. Alarms wailed. The control panel erupted with red lights. Technicians protected precious instruments with their bodies.

For a minute, it seemed all was lost. Next stop, the hard Earth.

Then, abruptly, the agitated air calmed. The engine caught its stride. Even before the helicopter stopped rocking, Karen's head was out the door, turning and peering frantically.

The first thing she saw was a pillar of smoke rising from flaming wreckage—an aircraft, probably one of the experimental fighter planes, lay in a crumpled heap at one end of a city street, with a trail of torn autos in its wake. That was awful enough. But she wasted no time turning the other way, to find—

—a pall of dust hanging over the part of town near Olympic and Rimpau, obscuring everything beneath. Out of this fog, the last few bits and flying components of the landing tripod could be seen rushing skyward, joining their fellows in the belly of the giant, hovering disk. Soon they were all recovered and the big hatch door began closing.

"What happened? What happened? What happened?"

For a moment Karen could not tell where the question came from. It was almost a simultaneous chant, emitted from her headphones, from everyone in the chopper, and from her own dazzled mind.

Then, as alien vessel started moving, an amplified voice took over the radio waves.

Thus, repayment is accomplished.
With this gift, the debt is erased.

Where the tripod had been, just minutes before, a stiffening breeze now tugged at the dust cloud, unravelling it—along with every shred of hope Karen had been vainly clutching. For under the clearing haze, she now saw that the whole area now lay empty.

Worse than empty.

The high school and several city blocks… were gone! Just a crater remained, circular, smooth-sided, and uniformly several meters deep.

A quiet, crystal clarity settled over Karen's senses. Over headphones she heard someone in authority shout a protest that was immediately translated into Garubis chatter-gabble.

"You call THIS a gift?"

The answer came almost immediately.

It is more than adequate, chosen from the
Wish List for Ambitious Upstarts.

Now we can wipe our feet clean of your dross.
When we next meet, it will be on our terms.

Earth's spokesman retorted in anger, speaking for a shocked human race.

"This meeting isn't over, you bastards. Nobody disintegrates our kids and gets away with it!"

Glittering reflections off metal. Angry jets converging, racing, kicked in their afterburners to catch up with the fast-receding alien craft... but Karen saw it was hopeless. All the fighter planes could do was launch a few missiles that streaked vengefully after the Garubis disk, then fell away as the vessel accelerated blithely, indifferently, toward space.

Karen had already dismissed the idea of revenge, at least for now. Tomorrow there would be work to do, analyzing what weapon had done this thing, and beginning the hard process of arming humankind for life in a hostile universe. A cosmos where the rules of honor were apparently far weirder than anybody imagined.

One where slaying a thousand adolescents was 'repayment' for an act of hospitality.

For now though, all she could do was stare at the steaming crater—its smooth floor now stained with liquids pouring from severed utility pipes. Water. Gasoline. Sewage. Soon, sparks from a broken electric line set the puddles ablaze.

Karen felt she could put out the flames with her tears.

Field Trip ⟨10⟩

A pall of dust filled the air, obscuring all sight of the towering tripod, the Garubis vessel... even the sky.

Even if the way had been clear, Mark wouldn't have seen much. Like everyone else, he was overwhelmed with nausea that lasted for several...

... seconds?

... minutes?

Something told him the confusion had stretched longer than that. Much longer—during the span between two breaths—while that brilliant, mind-numbing curtain poured down from the alien craft, tightening and coiling around them all...

What—he thought, feeling his chest heave for the next precious gasp of air.

When it finally came, with a wrenching half-sob, another shock hit him from a different place—his nasal cavities.

Smell!

Make that *smells*. A flood of unfamiliar aromas. Pungent, lush, sweet, tart, acrid, fatty, musty, fruity, reeking—and yet *none* of those things. There were strangenesses—frightening and intoxicating—in the very wind.

That was the first hint. Before his eyes could see or the ringing left his ears, an ancient portion of his brain knew, from smell alone. Something had changed, far more than a mere dust cloud.

What is it? Have they decided to kill us?

Determined to face it like a man, Mark forced his spine erect, waving away still-swirling puffs and blinking hard in order to clear away the spots. Lifting his face skyward in defiance, he raised a hand to shade his eyes...

...and saw nothing overhead but dissipating haze... and then clouds, rolling slowly across a blue sky.

The Garubis were gone, vanished, without a trace.

But it was the *shade* of blue overhead that unnerved him more than anything else. That, combined with the persistent, exotic aromas. Mark felt a chill climb his back as he lowered his gaze.

The haze began to clear.

"No," he sighed as shapes emerged.

Behind him stood the solid, reassuring bulk of Twenty-Nine Palms High School, with its broad front steps beneath his feet. Nearby, Alex, Barry and several dozen other students were gathering themselves after waves of nausea similar to his own. Further, beyond a stretch of lawn and a precariously tipping flag pole, stood Rimpau Avenue, a short row of small houses, then the Food King.

That is—half of Food King. Where the rest of the supermarket should have been, a wall of *forest* now stood. Trees, familiar in their pattern of branching limbs, but not in the wild colors of their leaves - crimson and lime. The nearest swayed and rippled from some recent disturbance. Several tipped over and crashed before Mark's unbelieving eyes.

"Are..." Mark swallowed. "Are you all right?" he asked Alexandra and Barry, helping them steady themselves, even as he turned to survey the forest verge. It swept in a perfect arc along one wall of the minimart, slicing Drannen's Hardware down the middle, then continued through Lovell Motors where the main row of cars had been reduced to steaming fragments.

"I think so," Alex answered. Barry gave a jerky nod, staring wide-eyed.

"Good. Come on then."

Mark started at a walk, as his friends recovered their balance. But in seconds it became a jog. Alex kept pace alongside as Mark went faster down the street, heading toward the nearest edge, feeling a sudden need to hurry. They took the last hundred meters at a run over cracked pavement, past a BMW with its alarm blaring, only stopping when they reached the rim of a sheer, five-meter drop. There, they stared down at an injured meadow that hissed and groaned in complaint.

Well, you'd feel wounded too, if someone dropped part of an American town on top of you, he thought, numbly.

One surviving tree pushed a clumpy spray of multicolored leaves near enough to touch. He reached toward it.

"Careful," Alex said. "All of this may be poisonous." She gestured at the forest, the clearings, and expanse of rolling hills that now lay before them, falling gently toward an azure-tangerine lake.

Mark quashed a sudden, hysterical urge to laugh. Somehow, he doubted the Garubis would go to all this trouble if the dangers were so simple or instantly overwhelming here. Wherever *here* was.

Oh, there were perils, almost certainly. But Na-bistaka's folk operated according to some kind of code, one that limited their viciousness. There would be a chance, if a slim one.

Out of stunned silence, a babble began to rise. *Two* babbles, actually. One ahead of him, as the forest began stirring again. No animal had yet shown itself, but he could hear local creatures rustling, getting over their surprise.

But a louder clamor came from behind—the loud and unreserved voices of Americans, who had never learned—till now—any of the art of prudence. How or when to be quiet. They came spilling out of the High School and other places of shelter, staring at the off-blue sky, the strangely too-yellow sun, the circle of gaudy forest and a range of snow-capped, serrated mountains that could be seen rising in the distance, far beyond the truncated athletic field.

"They sent us to some faraway planet!" Barry murmured. "They promised us a gift. Instead they *punished* us!"

"No." Alex shook her head, pausing a moment, staring at the beautiful strangeness. When she next spoke, her voice was hoarse but clear. "They may be spiteful devils, but you *can* call this a gift."

When Mark grunted in agreement, Barry cast him a questioning look.

"A colony," he explained, unable to utter more.

"C-colony?"

"Another world for humanity," Alex summed up, "if we manage to survive."

"A colony," Mark said again, letting the word sink in, and realizing that—crazy as it sounded—it must be true.

"Of course, they might've *told* us!" Alex murmured bitterly

Mark nodded. No kidding.

Given six days warning, a nation and world could have organized any number of volunteers, sorted by skill and profession, outfitted with every tool, ready for any contingency. Just a little advance notice would have allowed humanity a chance to gather its brightest and best-trained adults, ready to create a settlement. One equipped to study a new world, to come to terms with it, and to thrive.

But the Garubis didn't give notice. Instead, those arrogant space-jerks, without warning, chose to transport—

He looked around at his companions-in-exile. A thousand California teenagers, a hundred or so teachers and townsfolk, some carnival workers, a bag lady or two, all of them wandering in a fog of confusion and disbelief.

It's a gift. Chosen from that 'list' they mentioned, because some law or tradition required that they repay a debt they owed.

They had to give us something valuable...

...but they twisted the rules.

Na-bistaka—that nasty—must have done this as a joke, certain that we'll fail.

And we may fail. We may.

His jaw clenched hard.

But not if I have anything to say about it.

Mark turned to Alexandra, who looked very young and yet somehow steadier than any of the adults who could be seen right now, babbling in the street.

"We better hurry," he said. "There's a lot to do."

end of Book One

AFterword

This near-future "what if" tale of adolescent life and extraterrestrial adventure began circulating—in early drafts—way back during the nineteen-eighties. Distracted by other, more pressing projects, I would sometimes let teachers pass it around to their classes, asking "What do you think the author will do next?" or "What would you do next?" Many fun discussions ensued.

The strange quandary of "neotenous" modern youth... the intense frustration of being kept a child long after any other society would have let you be a grown woman or man... has long fascinated me, ever since my own time as an inmate in high school. Who doesn't dream of dramatic escape, during those years? Especially to some time and place where your skills and talent and character would really matter? That notion was developed, in another scenario, by my DAVID BRIN'S OUT OF TIME series, wherein three Nebula Award winning writers created brilliant little novels based on a premise somewhat similar to Sky Horizon. (Individual, troubled teens from our time get snatched away to have exciting adventures three hundred years in the future.)

Finally, after receiving many letters across two decades, I found an excellent collaborator—a rising star of SF named Jeff Carlson—to join with me in giving the Colony High project fresh momentum. The part that I had already finished—Sky Horizon— is what you hold right now. Jeff and I should get the next exciting installment to you pretty soon. Stay bold and open-minded!